VOTE FOR LOVE

"How could I have been so foolish? How could this have happened to me?" Viola asked herself desperately as she looked at the grim prison walls surrounding her.

Her only chance for release lay with the man she loved. Surely his influence could free her.

But suppose Rayburn decided to leave her there, she wondered in panic? Her suffragette activities and now her scandalous arrest could ruin his political career.

"He might never forgive me!" she cried, as tears flooded her eyes.

Even confinement in prison was preferable to the loss of Rayburn's love!

BARBARA CARTLAND

Bantam Books by Barbara Cartland
Ask your bookseller for the books you have missed

Barbara Cartland
Vote for Love

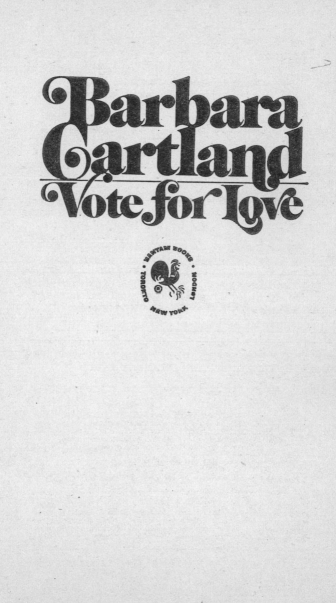

BANTAM BOOKS · TORONTO · NEW YORK · LONDON

VOTE FOR LOVE
A Bantam Book / February 1977

ISBN 0–553–10341–5

Published simultaneously in the United States and Canada

Bantam Books are published by Bantam Books, Inc. Its trade-
mark, consisting of the words "Bantam Books" and the por-
trayal of a bantam, is registered in the United States Patent
Office and in other countries. Marca Registrada, Bantam
Books, Inc., 666 Fifth Avenue, New York, New York 10019.

PRINTED IN THE UNITED STATES OF AMERICA

AUTHOR'S NOTE

After the return of the Liberals in 1906 the succeeding years saw the defeat of seven Women's Suffrage Bills. But the Militants grew more and more aggressive. They opposed the Government at every by-election, chained themselves to the railings in Downing Street, and continued their hunger-strikes in prison.

A woman tried to attack Winston Churchill with a dog-whip, another injured Lloyd George by throwing a steel spike at him in a cab. A bomb in Mr. Asquith's house in the country wrecked four rooms. Two railway stations went up in flames, and a bomb was found under the Bishop's chair in St. Paul's Cathedral.

On Derby Day, June 4, 1913, with the Suffragette colours sewn inside her coat, Emily Wilding Davidson threw herself in front of the galloping horses. She brought down the King's horse and died of her injuries.

After the war, the vote, which had been so bitterly fought for, was in 1918 granted without a struggle to married women, women householders, and women University graduates of over thirty.

CHAPTER ONE

1907

"I did not expect to get away so soon."

"Nor did I. The Prime Minister's decision to have a snap Division caught the Opposition off their guard and saved me from making a speech."

The sound of the footsteps of the two Members of Parliament walking through Westminster Hall seemed to echo round the ancient building.

"You were lucky, Lyle," the elder man remarked with a smile, "but then that is your reputation."

It was true that the Honourable Rayburn Lyle was known as "Lucky Lyle," although he disliked being reminded of it.

"It makes me feel like a jockey, or a trickster of some sort," he had said often enough.

At the same time, he was undeniably lucky.

Good-looking, extremely rich, and a member of an old and respected family, he had through sheer brilliance and intelligence become the Under-Secretary of State for Foreign Affairs before he was thirty-four.

When the new Liberal Government had come into power the previous year, the Prime Minister, Sir Henry Campbell-Bannerman, had given him a post which everyone agreed was well deserved.

At the same time, there were naturally those who thought he had risen up the political ladder too quickly and were envious.

Rayburn Lyle might have been resented more if

he had not had a sense of humour which enabled him
to laugh at himself.

There was something autocratic and a little un-
approachable about him which made people eye him
rather warily on first acquaintance.

But then he would smile and they would find
themselves swept away by his unmistakable charm.

"Can I give you a lift?" he asked now as he and
his companion reached the court-yard under Big Ben.

It was filled with carriages and a number of electric broughams, which many Members found useful
when in London.

"No, thank you," his friend answered. "I have my
own carriage and I am going to the Reform Club."

"I am going home," Rayburn Lyle replied.

His electric brougham came gliding quietly to
where they stood and the door was opened by an
attendant wearing the uniform of the House of Commons.

Rayburn Lyle stepped in and sat back against the
cushioned seat with a sigh of relief.

He had not looked forward to the speech he had
been expected to make in the debate on Foreign Affairs, because he had been asked by the Foreign Sec-
retary, Sir Edward Grey, to express not his own
views but those of the party, with which he was not
entirely in agreement.

The brougham set off.

As it passed through the gates of the court-yard
he heard cheers, shouts, and boos, and bent forward.
Outside St. Stephen's entrance he saw, as he expected, a demonstration.

It did not surprise him that it concerned the
Suffragettes.

They had been growing unceasingly more aggressive in the past year, and outside the House of
Commons they were a familiar sight with their
banners, their posters, and their leaflets, all inscribed
with: *Votes for Women!*

An alternative was the slogan *Vote against the*

Liberal Government! because it was well known that the Cabinet was almost solidly against them.

Mr. Herbert Asquith, the Chancellor of the Exchequer, had in fact stated publicly that he was not in favour of Women's Suffrage.

Rayburn Lyle had not yet made up his mind at all firmly.

The women with whom he concerned himself—and there were a large number of them—were not interested in votes but in love and in himself in particular.

As an extremely eligible bachelor, he was pursued by match-making mothers, but he found young girls a bore and devoted himself to the alluring, sophisticated, fascinating beauties whom the King also found so delightful.

Rayburn Lyle was at the moment having an *affaire de coeur* with Lady Davenport.

Eloise Davenport was one of the great beauties of the period.

She was acclaimed not only by her own social set but also by the popular Press.

Post-cards portraying her flashing dark eyes and raven-black hair, her capacious bosom and tiny eighteen-inch waist, were on sale together with those of the other so-called Professional Beauties.

These included the Countess of Dudley, Lady Randolph Churchill, and Mrs. Cornwallis West, besides musical-comedy actresses like Camille Clifford—the Gibson Girl Gertie Miller, and Gabrielle Ray.

It was Eloise Davenport who Rayburn Lyle was thinking of as his brougham proceeded through Parliament Square towards Queen Anne's Gate, where he had a London house within convenient reach of the House of Commons.

It was not yet eight o'clock, but since his early return was unexpected he thought that it would be too late for him to order dinner at home, and that when he had changed his clothes he would be well advised to dine at one of his Clubs.

It was so unusual for him to have an evening free that he found himself wondering in some perplexity how to make the best of it.

He had been certain when he left his house after luncheon that it would be the early hours of the morning before he saw it again.

"I will go to the St. James," he decided, remembering that two of his closest friends had said they would be dining there.

After a good meal, such as the St. James invariably supplied, they could play billiards or cards, although gambling for high stakes always rather bored him.

As the brougham drew up at his front door Rayburn Lyle drew his latch-key from his pocket.

The servants would not be expecting him and would certainly be downstairs in the basement, so that it would take longer to ring the bell and wait for an answer than to let himself in.

"I will leave again in half an hour," he told his chauffeur.

"Very good, Sir," the man replied.

Rayburn Lyle walked up the steps and opened the door. As he expected, the house was very quiet and seemed to be deserted.

Having put his hat down on the hall-table, he walked to his study at the back of the house, carrying a brief-case containing a number of State papers which must be locked up before he went out to dinner.

He thought as he was thirsty that he would have a drink before he rang the bell for his valet and went upstairs to change.

The dry, moistureless atmosphere of the Chamber always gave him a thirst.

He opened the door of the Study, then was frozen into immobility by sheer astonishment.

On the hearth-rug in front of the mantelpiece there was a woman crouching down with her hands over her face, and beside her was an object which Rayburn Lyle immediately identified as a bomb!

Even as he stared it began to hiss and emit sparks, and as it did so the woman who was cowering beside it looked round as if she had sensed rather than heard his entrance.

Slowly, almost reluctantly it seemed, she began to rise to her feet, and Rayburn Lyle acted.

Dropping his brief-case on the floor, he ran forward and seizing the woman pulled her roughly behind the sofa. Then flinging her down on the floor he threw himself on top of her.

The bomb was hissing ominously, and now, although he could not see it, protected as he was by the back of the sofa, Rayburn Lyle was sure that it was emitting more sparks and it was only a question of seconds before it exploded.

He wondered if there was anything more he could do, any better protection he could find from the devastation which he knew the explosion would create.

However, it would be foolish to move now and he could only keep his head down, hoping as he did so that he would not be maimed or injured as other victims of bomb outrages had been.

Still nothing happened and after a moment he was conscious that the woman beneath him was lying face downwards and that her body was very soft.

She must have lost her hat as he pulled her from the hearth-rug and he could see that her hair was pale brown in colour, curling in little tendrils at the nape of her neck.

He suspected that she was holding her breath, as he was, waiting for the moment when the whole room would rock and the ceiling might come down on their heads.

They waited.

Listening, it seemed to Rayburn Lyle that the hissing had stopped and after a moment he said:

"When was it timed to go off?"

He felt a little quiver go through her at the sound of his voice. Then she said hesitatingly:

"It . . . should have . . . exploded by . . . now."

"Then why the hell were you kneeling beside it?" he enquired.

She did not reply.

Cautiously, because he had no wish to have his face blown off, he peeped over the top of the sofa to see the bomb lying somewhat forlornly on the hearth-rug.

There were no longer any sparks, only a powdered mess on the carpet round it.

"Stay where you are!" Rayburn Lyle ordered.

Rising tentatively to his feet, he moved still with his eyes on the bomb to the table in the corner of the room, where there was a tray containing drinks.

As he expected, there were not only decanters and glasses but also a large jug of lemonade, which he often preferred when he was thirsty.

He picked it up and moving warily towards the bomb poured the lemonade over it.

There was no sound, not even the hiss of dying embers.

He put the jug down on the side-table and said harshly:

"You can come out now. It is quite safe."

For a moment he thought the woman could not have heard him. Then she rose and he saw himself looking at a very frightened face which at the same time he had to admit was unusually beautiful.

She had small delicate features which were difficult to notice because they were eclipsed by two very large, frightened eyes that were surprisingly almost purple in their depths.

She seemed very young and there was something child-like about her as she said in a helpless little voice which seemed to be caught on the verge of tears:

"I . . . am . . . sorry."

"Sorry that you have not caused any damage?" Rayburn Lyle asked severely.

"S-sorry . . . it has made such a . . . mess," she replied inconsequentially.

"It would have been a far worse mess if it had done what it was intended to do," he said, "and you would undoubtedly have been killed."

He saw a sudden flicker in her eyes and added incredulously:

"You meant to kill yourself! That is why you were crouching beside it when you thought it was about to go off!"

She did not answer and after a moment he asked sharply:

"Tell me the truth. Did you mean to die?"

"Y-yes.!"

He could hardly hear her answer, and yet there was no doubt that it was in the affirmative.

"Good God!" he exclaimed. "Are there no lengths to which you women will not go to make fools of yourselves?"

He looked at her contemptuously as he spoke.

"Can you really be so idiotic as to believe that by wrecking my house and killing yourself it would take you one single step nearer to getting the vote?"

As if the anger in his voice broke her self-control, tears came into the woman's eyes as she said again:

"I am ... sorry ... very, very ... sorry."

Rayburn Lyle looked at her, then walked towards the door.

"Well, I had better fetch the Police. That, I suppose, is what you want—to make a martyr of yourself one way or the other."

"No ... please ... please do not send me to ... prison."

There was a frantic note of fear in her plea which arrested him.

He turned round.

"Surely that is all part of the plan?" he asked. "You refuse to pay the imposed fine, you are sent to prison, go on a hunger-strike, and have the National Press denouncing the cruelty and inhumanity of the Government."

The woman gave a little sob.

"I cannot . . . go to . . . prison . . . I cannot! That is . . . why I was . . . trying to . . . kill myself!"

She looked at the unexploded bomb and made a pathetic little gesture with her hands.

"I am so . . . hopeless," she said. "I am a . . . failure . . . even at dying."

Rayburn Lyle walked back towards her.

"Perhaps you would like to tell me what all this is about," he said in a very different tone of voice. "I admit to finding it extremely bewildering."

She looked up at him, her large eyes filled with tears, her lips trembling, and he thought he had never seen anyone who was quite so lovely in an unusual way.

She was not in the least like any of the girls he had seen at Society gatherings.

There was in fact something not only very young and innocent about her, but also something sensitive and spiritual that he had not noticed in a woman for a very long time.

It was this that made him say in a far kinder tone than he had used before:

"Sit down and tell me what all this is about. I expect you would like a drink. I know I need one."

He walked to the drink-tray and without asking her preference opened a half-bottle of champagne that lay in the wine-cooler and poured out a glass.

He handed it to her, then poured himself a glass and sipped the wine appreciatively, feeling that his throat was even dryer than it had been when he left the House of Commons.

"Sit down," he ordered, "and I suggest you start by telling me your name."

She hesitated, as if she thought it would be best to remain anonymous. Then dropping her eyes she answered:

"My name is Viola . . . Brandon."

"Brandon?" Rayburn Lyle repeated. "Then of course you must be related to Lady Brandon, who is one of the leaders of your Movement."

"She is my Stepmother."

"I knew your father," Rayburn Lyle said. "I cannot believe that he would wish you to behave in this outrageous manner."

"Papa would have . . . hated it!"

Rayburn Lyle was surprised that she admitted it, but it was undoubtedly the truth.

Sir Richard Brandon had been one of the most respected and beloved Gentlemen-in-Waiting to Queen Victoria.

He would have been, Rayburn Lyle was sure, appalled at his daughter's being a Suffragette when those strident and outrageous women were making a considerable nuisance of themselves in their efforts to command attention.

"If you know that your father would have disapproved of your action," he said sternly, "why did you do it?"

"I have . . . tried to refuse," Viola said with a little sob, "but my . . . Stepmother will not listen. She is . . . fanatical on the subject."

Rayburn Lyle knew this was the truth.

Allying herself with Mrs. Pankhurst and Mrs. Pethwick-Lawrence, Lady Brandon was making speeches up and down the country, and by every possible method that she and her colleagues could think up keeping the Movement firmly on the front pages of the newspapers.

"Are you telling me that your Stepmother forces you to do this sort of thing against your will?"

Viola drew in her breath and it was almost a sob.

"I am a . . . coward," she said after a moment. "I am . . . afraid of going to . . . prison . . . I am not . . . brave like the . . . other women. . . . I am terrified . . . really terrified of being . . . forcibly fed!"

There was a note of horror in her voice that was unmistakable and Rayburn Lyle could see that as she spoke her fingers interlocked on her lap and were trembling.

"Surely if you tell your Stepmother what you feel in this matter she cannot compel you to . . ."

He stopped suddenly.

He saw the terror in Viola's eyes as she raised them to his.

It was an expression he had never seen in a woman's face before and it made the words he had been about to say die on his lips.

"This is ridiculous!" he said sharply. "If you do defy her, what can she do about it?"

"She will . . . beat me," Viola said almost beneath her breath.

Rayburn Lyle stared at her in amazement, hardly believing he had heard her aright.

It was not so surprising that a woman should be beaten; that was commonplace enough. Fathers whipped their sons, who were even more rigorously flogged at their Public Schools, and often meted out the same punishment to recalcitrant daughters.

But it surprised and indeed shocked him that Lady Brandon, who had an established place in Society, should beat anyone so obviously sensitive as her stepdaughter.

"She has not beaten me so . . . frequently since I . . . grew up," Viola said hastily, "but she often whipped me after she married Papa, mostly I think because she was not as happy with him as she had expected to be."

Rayburn Lyle acknowledged the intelligence of the remark.

At the same time, he remembered that Sir Richard had been getting on in age when he married for the second time, while Lady Brandon was comparatively a young woman.

Remembering her as large and aggressive-looking, he could understand that she found this small, flower-like creature an irritant on whom she could wreak her own frustrations.

"I can understand your being frightened of your Stepmother," he said aloud, "but there is a great difference between being frightened and trying to destroy yourself."

"I told you I was a . . . coward," Viola said miserably.

She sipped a little of the champagne and now she set the glass down on the table beside the sofa.

"Are you still going to . . . send for the . . . Police?" she asked apprehensively.

"If I did so I should feel that I too had committed a crime," he answered.

He saw a sudden light in her eyes.

"Thank you," she said. "But I shall have to tell my Stepmother that the bomb did not . . . go off, and she will be very . . . angry with me."

"How could it be your fault?" Rayburn Lyle enquired.

"I . . . I altered the timer."

She gave him a glance from under her eyelashes as she went on:

"They expected you to be at the House of Commons until late tonight. This had been announced, and they set the bomb to go off after you had returned home. I was to hide it somewhere in the room where you would not see it."

"How did you get in—as a matter of interest?"

"One of my Stepmother's friends lifted me over the railings of your garden at the back of the house," she answered. "They showed me how to open the window with a pen-knife and when I was inside I closed it again."

She glanced towards the window as she spoke.

"I had no idea it was so easy for burglars or anyone else to break in," Rayburn Lyle said ruefully. "I must have more-efficient locks fitted to the windows in future."

"I think you ought to do that," Viola agreed seriously, "and it was not really difficult to climb over the railings with the help of someone else."

"Your instructions were to hide the bomb?"

"I was then told to let myself out the front door as soon as there was no-one about," Viola said. "But because I knew that if I was successful with this bomb I would have to do all sorts of other horrible things, I thought the only thing I could do was die when this one went off!"

"I cannot imagine how you could contemplate such a wicked action!" Rayburn Lyle said. "You are young. You have your whole life in front of you. How could you run away from your responsibilities in such a reprehensible manner?"

She gave a sigh which seemed to come from the very depths of her being.

"Papa would have been . . . ashamed of me, but I thought he would understand."

"I understand. But you have to be brave enough to stand up to your Stepmother," Rayburn Lyle said. "Have you no relatives with whom you could live?"

"I do not think anyone would want me, and even if they did she would not let me go," Viola replied. "You see . . . she thinks I am . . . an asset."

"In what way?"

"I am Papa's daughter and if the bomb was successful my Stepmother was going to announce that it was I who planted it in your house. I would be arrested and im . . . imprisoned."

The last word was obviously hard to say and Rayburn Lyle realised how terrified she was of the thought of prison. It did not surprise him.

The horrors of what the women endured because they deliberately chose to be martyred for their Cause were splashed over every newspaper.

There were a number of reporters who found it good copy to describe in detail the disgusting process of being forcibly fed through the nostril.

Also the violence which they averred the Suffragettes encountered at the hands of the Police who were not sympathetic to their Cause was most graphically reported.

It would have been frightening for any well-bred woman, but he could imagine the agonies it could evoke in someone as sensitive as Viola.

"We shall have to think of a convincing explanation of what happened," he said, "one which will protect you from being blamed for the failure of the bomb and bring no retribution on your head."

Viola looked hopefully at him and after a moment he went on:

"I think the best thing would be for you to say that you planted the bomb as arranged and left the house without anyone seeing you.

"When you arrive home and nothing happens and there are no reports of any damage, then your Step-mother will simply assume that the bomb was discovered and defused without the Police being involved in the matter."

"Could I . . . really do that?" Viola asked.

"I see no reason why anyone should be suspicious that you were involved in the bomb being faulty," Rayburn Lyle said.

"Oh, thank you . . . thank you!"

There was no mistaking the gratitude in her voice or the faint colour that had returned to her cheeks.

"At the same time," he said, "you must try not to do this sort of thing again."

"How can I help it?" she asked. "My Stepmother is determined I shall support the Cause. She tells me that I am hopeless and inefficient and my only value lies in the fact that I am Papa's daughter."

She was silent for a moment, then she added:

"You had much better have left me to . . . die. I was not half so afraid when I was waiting for the bomb to go off as I am now . . . wondering what is the next thing she will . . . make me . . . do."

"Perhaps it will not be as bad as you think."

He spoke automatically, but he realised immediately after saying the words that it sounded as if he was washing his hands of her troubles and was no longer interested in them.

It was her sensitivity, he thought, that made her say quickly:

"I am sorry that I am keeping you so . . . long when you must be wanting your dinner. Please forgive me . . . and thank you for being so . . . kind."

As she spoke, she bent to pick up her hat from where it lay on the floor.

It was a rather inappropriate head-gear, Rayburn Lyle thought, for the dastardly deed she had set out to do.

A wide-brimmed straw trimmed with a wreath of white roses, it was the hat of a girl, and when she put it on it made her appear even younger.

Her dress was expensive and fitted her slim figure and tiny waist, which he was sure owed nothing to the tight lacing that other women found so necessary.

There was a grace about her as she stood ready to leave that reminded him of a gazelle or one of the young deer which grazed beneath the oak trees in the Park of his house in the country.

Viola put out her hand and as he took it in his, her fingers felt very cold.

"How are you going to get home?" he asked.

"I will find a hackney carriage," she answered. "There is sure to be one in Parliament Square."

He frowned.

It seemed to him inconceivable that Lady Brandon should allow anyone so young and lovely to walk about the streets unchaperoned at this hour of the night.

The older Suffragettes might fancy themselves emancipated and free from conventional restrictions, but Viola was obviously quite incapable of looking after herself.

"I will send you back in my brougham," he said. "It is outside. Where do you live?"

"In Curzon Street," she answered. "But . . . please, you must not worry about ↘ . . . me. I will be all right."

"I will send you home," he said firmly.

"It is very kind of you," Viola answered, "but would you please ask your chauffeur to stop a little lower down the street? I would not wish my Stepmother to know that I had met you."

"Yes, of course," Rayburn Lyle replied, "you are being very sensible. But promise me one thing. . . ."

He still held her hand in his and she made no effort to take it from him.

"What do you want me to . . . promise?" she asked.

Her eyes were a little apprehensive and he thought again that they seemed almost purple in their depths and were singularly appropriate to her name.

She was like a violet, gentle, shy, ready to hide away under protective leaves, with no wish to face the harshness of the world outside.

"Promise me," he insisted, "that you will never again attempt to take your own life."

Just for a moment she hesitated. Then as if he compelled her to answer she said:

"I . . . promise!"

"You must try to stand up to your Stepmother, however harshly she treats you. It will be better than being sent to prison."

"Yes . . . I know," Viola agreed, "but when she threatens me I am so . . . foolish and . . . cowardly that I . . . agree to anything she . . . suggests."

Her head dropped as she murmured:

"I am . . . afraid of pain. I know I ought to be . . . brave, but I am . . . not."

"You must try," Rayburn Lyle said firmly. "But whatever happens, you have given me your promise and I feel sure you will not break it."

"No . . . I will not break it," she murmured.

He opened the door and they walked into the Hall.

As they reached the front door she looked up at him.

"You have been so . . . kind," she said. "It is difficult to say thank you. But I shall never . . . forget you."

He smiled at her. Just for a moment they looked into each other's eyes and he thought that hers seemed to widen and become even bigger than they were already.

Then he opened the door and accompanied her to his brougham, which was waiting outside.

"Take this lady to the end of Curzon Street,"

Rayburn Lyle ordered the chauffeur. "Then return for me."

"Very good, Sir."

Viola stepped in and there was just a glimpse of a lace-trimmed petticoat showing beneath the hem of her skirt, and a very small foot in a glacé kid slipper.

Then the door was shut, the brougham moved off, and Rayburn Lyle walked back into the house.

He told himself that it had been the most fantastic encounter he had ever had with a woman.

He walked back into the Study and stood looking at the mess on the hearth-rug.

How could he have imagined when he returned home from the House of Commons what he would find waiting for him? Anyway, the first thing to do was to have it cleared up.

As he pealed the bell for the servants he decided that he would make sure in future that no-one could enter his house so easily.

* * *

The electric brougham deposited Viola as ordered at the bottom of Curzon Street and she walked quickly along the pavement to her Stepmother's house with its high steps and gold-tipped railings.

It was Lady Brandon's money which had provided them a far larger and more impressive residence than they had been able to afford when her mother was alive.

Viola had often wondered if one of the reasons which had made her father marry again was that he had so little money and it had always been a struggle to make ends meet.

But the idea of marriage had come not from Sir Richard, Viola felt certain, but from a woman called Mavis Selby.

She had made up her mind to marry Sir Richard from the first moment they met, and it had finally been weakness rather than any ardent desire which had taken him up the aisle.

Perhaps, Viola had ruminated later, he had been

thinking of her, feeling that a motherless daughter of eleven years old was too much for him to cope with.

But from the moment her Stepmother took charge of her life she had been miserably unhappy in a manner that was hard to describe to any outsider.

Ever since childhood Viola had been aware of the closeness that existed between her father and mother and herself. It had been a part of their love that was inexpressible in words.

It was just that they belonged together and everything they thought and said was somehow interesting and became part of the sheer happiness of living.

When her mother died, that was lost, and she thought later that something in her father had died too. Three years after she had followed her mother to the graveside she watched his coffin being lowered into the ground.

Then there was only her Stepmother left—a strident, overpowering woman who had resented and disliked her from the very moment they first met.

Viola was intelligent enough to understand that she was everything that her Stepmother deprecated in her own sex.

She was gentle, ineffectual, and only too willing to have everything decided for her by someone she thought wiser and more intelligent.

In her case, after her mother's death it had been her father, and she could not understand why her Stepmother continually tried to make her oppose his decisions or argue against his wishes.

Later she realised that this was mainly simple jealousy, but it was also fundamentally part of Lady Brandon's character that she would not be subservient to any man, whoever he might be.

Ostensibly she was a woman who hated men and their superiority.

Her weakness lay in the fact that she wanted men to desire her as a woman, yet loathed men with a bitter, resentful hatred when her behaviour outraged them.

She had been over thirty when she married, and in fact Sir Richard had seemed her last chance of finding herself a husband.

She was well-endowed financially, but the men who might have been prepared to accept her for her money found that her aggressiveness and her manner of being ready to attack them on any subject that concerned the female sex was almost repulsive.

She was however clever enough, once she was Lady Brandon, to accept the position in Society that she was accorded not only by her husband's connections at Court but also because of his popularity.

Everyone loved Sir Richard and his friends decided that if it made him happy to marry a woman whom they personally disliked, then they would make the best of her for his sake.

But since his death Viola realised that the good-will he had engendered for his wife was wearing thin, although there were still people who welcomed Viola into their homes because she was her father's daughter.

Viola also knew, although they were too tactful to say so, that they felt sorry for her because she had to live with her Stepmother.

In a way, she thought as she walked into the house, she did not miss her father so acutely here in Curzon Street as she would have done if they were still living in Onslow Square, their home where she had been so happy.

The servant who let her in informed her that her Stepmother was in the Drawing-Room, and with feet that seemed suddenly to be as heavy as lead and a frightened fluttering of her heart Viola went slowly up the stairs.

The long elegant Drawing-Room with three windows overlooking the street was well furnished and contained some valuable pictures which Lady Brandon had brought with her on her marriage.

But Viola as she entered the room had eyes only for her Stepmother, who was sitting at a desk at the far end, writing out, she knew without asking, notes and memoranda for the meetings she was planning.

Lady Brandon looked up as her stepdaughter entered and her eyes were cold as she asked sharply:

"Well? What happened?"

"I . . . I left the . . . bomb as you . . . told me to do."

"Good!" Lady Brandon answered. "Well, you had better get something to eat, then go to bed. If the announcement of the explosion is in the morning papers, I will make it known that you were responsible, then you will be arrested."

With an effort Viola put up her chin.

"I do not wish to be . . . arrested, *Madre*."

Madre was the Spanish for "Mother" and Lady Brandon had chosen it when as a child Viola had refused point blank to call her "Mama" or "Mother" in English.

"Do not be so absurd!" Lady Brandon said in an irritated tone. "The whole point of placing the bomb in the house of the Under-Secretary of State was for the publicity."

"I do not think . . . Papa would have wished me to have that sort of . . . publicity."

Viola was trembling but her voice was quite steady.

"Your father is not here to support your contention. So whatever he might have thought if he were alive, you will do as I say."

"I cannot go to . . . prison!" Viola said. "Please let me . . . pay the . . . fine."

Lady Brandon's lips tightened.

"I should think in this case it is unlikely they will give you the option, so the question will not arise," she replied. "But if you shame me in front of my friends by refusing to follow their heroic example, then I promise you that you will pay for it in a different manner!"

There was no mistaking the threat in her voice and Viola went very pale.

Then she felt that nothing was to be gained at

this moment by defying her Stepmother, when she knew that the Police in fact would not be called in.

She turned to leave the room.

As she did so Lady Brandon looked at her with that unmistakable expression of dislike.

"If you are going to defy me, Viola," she said, "I promise you, you will be sorry. You are privileged, and I mean that word, to take part in the greatest crusade in which women have ever been involved. You should be grateful for the chance—very grateful!"

Viola did not reply and Lady Brandon said almost violently:

"Do not stand there looking half-witted. Go to bed and get out of my sight. You are a typical example of a feminine slave subservient to the caprices of men and you infuriate me!"

Viola recognised the phrases that Lady Brandon used so tellingly on public platforms.

She had nothing to reply and leaving the Drawing-Room she proceeded up the stairs to her bedroom.

She was not hungry and had no wish to eat. She just wanted to be alone.

When she reached her bed-room she pulled off her hat and flung herself down on the bed, hiding her face in the pillow.

"Oh, Papa," she whispered. "How can I bear it? How can I go on living like this?"

Even as she spoke she remembered her promise to Rayburn Lyle.

She could see the expression in his eyes and feel the warm strength of his fingers.

"He is kind," she told herself, "kind and . . . understanding. Why should I hate someone like that just because he is a . . . man?"

CHAPTER TWO

Lady Brandon came into the Library with a large box of leaflets in her arms. She set them down with a bang on the table and looked across the room at Viola.

The Library had been Sir Richard's special sanctum and was filled with his books, which no-one opened now except his daughter.

There were big leather arm-chairs which had come from their previous home in Onslow Square, and the rest of the furniture consisted also of pieces that Viola remembered since she was a child.

Whenever she was in the Library, she somehow felt as if it was a violation of privacy when her Step-mother entered it.

"I cannot think what has happened," Lady Brandon said. "Christabel Pankhurst has looked at Rayburn Lyle's house from the front and the back and there is no sign of any damage."

Viola said nothing, but her eyes as she watched her Stepmother's face were wary.

"All I can think," Lady Brandon went on, "is that they discovered the bomb before it was due to explode. You could not have hidden it at all well."

Still Viola did not speak and Lady Brandon said contemptuously:

"It is what I might have expected! You bungle everything you do. You are without exception the most incompetent fool with whom I have ever had any dealings!"

She pushed the box of leaflets farther on the table and went on:

"What you can do now instead of wasting your time reading is to count these leaflets into packets of one hundred. Try not to make a mess of that!"

Viola walked towards the table.

"We are both asked to the Marchioness of Roe-hamptons's 'At Home' this afternoon," Lady Brandon continued. "I expected to have to go alone, but if by any fortunate chance you are arrested while we are there, it would certainly cause a sensation."

"I think it would be very . . . embarrassing," Viola said in a low voice.

"Embarrassment is what I feel as you go on making mistakes and messing up the easiest assignments," Lady Brandon said sharply. "I am quite certain that Mrs. Pankhurst already questions your enthusiasm."

"Then perhaps it would be better for me to do nothing in future," Viola said, "except perhaps do some of the writing for you and arrange the leaflets."

The words died away as she saw the expression on her Stepmother's face.

"I have told you before what a contribution you can make to our crusade. Your father is still remembered, and as his daughter you have a certain news value."

"It seems . . . wrong to use Papa's name now that he is . . . dead," Viola murmured.

But her Stepmother was not listening to her. Instead, she went out of the Library and slammed the door behind her.

Viola gave a sigh of relief.

Things had turned out better than she had anticipated.

Her Stepmother had in fact not suspected that she might have played an active part in preventing the bomb from exploding, and although she was abusive and contemptuous Viola told herself that hard words were easier to bear than the terror of being imprisoned.

When she had finished the task that had been set her, she began to look forward to visiting the Marchioness of Roehampton.

The old lady had been a friend of her father and she was the one hostess in London whose parties were enjoyable because she mixed her guests indiscriminately.

Artists, writers, musicians, even theatrical personalities rubbed shoulders with the cream of the nobility in her huge Reception-Rooms.

The Marchioness had been a character all her life and she was also important enough to do very much as she pleased.

The King and Queen honoured her with their friendship.

It was well known that King Edward found her parties amusing and was never as particular about the guests he met with the Marchioness as he was with some of the other hostesses who entertained him.

When Viola had finished sorting the leaflets and had eaten a quick luncheon with her Stepmother, she went upstairs to change into one of the attractive gowns which had been bought for her before the Season started.

They were nearly all in white; for young girls were expected to dress simply in white garments, which proclaimed their innocence. Not until they were married were bright colours and jewels permitted.

The gown into which Viola was helped by a lady's-maid was ornamented with *broderie anglaise,* which also edged the wide-brimmed hat.

She looked very young and very lovely as she followed in her Stepmother's wake up the wide staircase of Roehampton House to where the Marchioness was receiving.

There was a buzz of conversation coming from the big Reception-Rooms and an overpowering fragrance of hot-house flowers mingled with the exotic French perfume with which every woman was lavishly besprinkled.

"How nice to see you, Lady Brandon!" the Marchioness of Roehampton said conventionally.

But there was a smile of unmistakable welcome when she held out her hand to Viola.

"My child. I have been so looking forward to seeing you," she exclaimed. "I only wish your father could be here today."

"So do I," Viola answered.

"I must talk to you later," the Marchioness said as the Butler announced in stentorian tones the next guest

Viola did not know many of the people present, the majority of them being far older than she.

There were a few young girls looking rather dull and insignificant beside their glittering, sophisticated mothers with their exquisitely curved figures.

Viola recognised Lady Juliette Lowther, who was the Countess de Grey's only child.

She was tall like her mother, who was a famous beauty, but painfully shy, and she had been cruelly neglected.

Viola had heard many of her contemporaries whispering about her unhappy childhood.

The fact that Viola had no mother to chaperon her was something she regretted ever since she had "come out" the previous Season.

She was well aware that her mother would not have made her feel awkward and embarrassed, nor would she have been urged to marry just for the sake of acquiring a title.

When she was young her mother had often spoken of the manner in which the Duchess of Manchester had forced her daughters into marriage with three elder sons.

"The Duchess of Manchester is a hard mother," Viola heard her mother say once. "Her daughters have become emotionally frozen while she pursues her worldly successes."

"And the Marquess of Hartington," Sir Richard had added.

"Hush, not in front of Viola," her mother had said quickly.

The Duchess had married the Marquess after a liaison which had lasted thirty years and had become the Duchess of Devonshire.

Viola realised as she grew up that infidelity and a lack of matrimonial affection apparently reaped unexpected rewards.

Two or three older women spoke to her as she drank a cup of tea, and she was introduced to a débutante who was so painfully shy that she found it impossible to answer any of the remarks which were made to her.

Then as Viola was looking with interest at a collection of antique snuff-boxes in a glass case at the side of the room she heard the Marchioness of Roehampton's voice.

"Here you are, dear child!" she said. "I have been looking for you. The Earl of Croxdale has asked especially to be introduced to you."

Viola turned round hastily.

She felt perhaps it had been rude of her to have been preoccupied with her hostess's possessions rather than with her guests.

Standing beside the Marchioness, who was ablaze with diamonds and whose blue eyes were smiling at her affectionately, she saw what she considered to be a middle-aged man.

He was smartly dressed and had that inevitably autocratic presence which told her he was someone of importance.

"Lord Croxdale knew your father well," the Marchioness explained, "and your mother."

"She was very beautiful!" the Earl said.

Viola's eyes lit up. She was always thrilled to meet anyone who had known her mother, but with the lapse of time they were growing few and far between.

The Marchioness moved away to speak to someone else and the Earl said:

"Shall we find somewhere to sit down? I always find it hard to talk in such a crush."

"So do I," Viola answered, "and often it is difficult to hear what is being said."

"Then let us find somewhere quiet," the Earl suggested.

There was a door opening out of the main Reception-Room into another in which there were only a few people standing in groups, talking vivaciously.

Beyond that room there was another smaller room, exquisitely furnished in a more intimate manner, which made Viola suspect that it was in fact the Marchioness's *Boudoir*.

It was empty and the Earl said with satisfaction:

"This is better!"

He shut the door behind them and as Viola seated herself on a blue satin-covered sofa he sat down beside her.

"You knew my mother?" she asked eagerly. "Please tell me about her."

"She was, as I have already said, exquisitely beautiful," the Earl replied, "and you are very like her."

Viola flushed with pleasure.

"I like to think that," she said in a low voice.

"I assure you I am speaking truthfully, and because your father was a friend of mine, you and I must be friends."

There was a note in his voice which made Viola raise her eyes to his a little questioningly.

He seemed, she thought, much too old to be her friend, but because he had spoken so warmly of her mother she replied impulsively:

"I would like that, and please tell me more about Mama."

"I would rather talk about you."

Again Viola looked at the Earl in surprise.

He must, she thought, have been quite good-looking when he was young, but now there were deep lines under his eyes which gave him a somewhat debauched look.

Instinctively she felt as if she must draw away from him. He had not moved but she felt that he was encroaching upon her.

"Where did you first meet my father?" she asked hastily.

"Of course at Buckingham Palace, and he and your mother have stayed with me at my house in Oxfordshire."

"That must have been a long time ago."

"I met your father more frequently after he was widowed."

There was a silence for a moment. Then the Earl said:

"Tell me about yourself, Viola."

The fact that he used her Christian name on such short acquaintance seemed to Viola almost an impertinence.

Then she realised it was because he thought of her as a child, as she must have been when he had known her father and mother.

"There is very little to tell," she answered evasively.

"You are happy living with your Stepmother?"

"I miss Papa."

She had no idea how expressive her eyes were as she spoke.

"Of course you do," the Earl said, "and that is why I feel I must look after you."

Viola wondered what he was trying to say.

The Earl reached out and took her hand in his.

"What I am going to suggest," he said, "is that you come and stay at Croxdale Park next weekend. I shall have a house-party which I know will amuse you, and naturally your Stepmother is included in the invitation."

"That is very kind of you," Viola replied.

She did not know why but she felt uncomfortable because he was holding her hand and one of his fingers was caressing her palm.

"I . . . I think . . ." she began.

"I am also going to suggest," the Earl went on, "that you both dine with me tomorrow evening and we go to a theatre. I am sure you would enjoy seeing *The Merry Widow.*"

"Yes . . . I would like that," Viola replied.

At the same time, she tried to take her hand from his and found it impossible.

"Then that is agreed," the Earl said with satisfaction, "and I hope, little Viola, you are going to be as kind and sweet to me as I want you to be."

She did not know what to answer to this.

She felt even more uncomfortable than she had before at the intimate note in his voice and the proximity of his face to her own.

He looked at her for a long moment, then he lifted her hand and kissed it.

She felt his lips warm and possessive against her skin and she wished she had not taken off her gloves to eat the sandwiches and the little iced cakes which were offered to the guests.

"I suppose I should take you back to your Stepmother," the Earl said softly, "but if I had my way I would sit here saying many secret things into your adorable shell-like ear."

His face came even nearer and his eyes seemed to have almost a hypnotic expression in them. In a panic Viola rose quickly from the sofa.

"I am sure my Stepmother will be . . . wondering where I . . . am."

"She will know that you are safe with me," the Earl replied. "As I have already said, Viola, I will look after you."

Viola thought that that was the last thing she wanted, but because it was impossible to put her feelings into words she moved hurriedly towards the door.

She opened it before the Earl could reach her side.

"We will meet tomorrow night!" he said as they stepped into the next room. "I will arrange everything with your Stepmother. If she is too busy chaining herself to the railings or assaulting Members of Parliament, I will find you another Chaperon."

He spoke contemptuously and Viola knew he was not just laughing at her Stepmother but also sneering at her.

Although she hated everything the Suffragettes

did, she could not help feeling that it was bad manners on the part of a stranger to be so critical.

Her chin went up and she moved determinedly through the crowded room to where Lady Brandon was deep in conversation with an elderly man.

He looked like a rich financier. Viola was sure that that was what he actually was and her Stepmother was endeavouring to extract money from him.

Mrs. Pankhurst and her committee were always in need of money.

One of the reasons why Lady Brandon kept in regular touch with her social acquaintances was that this afforded the chance of meeting wealthy men like Baron Hirsch and Sir Ernest Cassel.

They could sometimes be badgered into giving her a cheque to help the Women's Suffrage Movement, even though they did not approve of it.

Viola knew that if her Stepmother was engaged on what she would consider "business" she would not wish to be interrupted.

She looked round hoping to see a familiar face, and as she did so she saw with a sudden start Rayburn Lyle shaking hands with their hostess.

Beside him was one of the most beautiful women Viola had ever seen. She thought in fact there was no-one in the room who could rival her, either in beauty or in *chic*.

Lady Davenport had in fact persuaded Rayburn Lyle against his will to accompany her to the Marchioness's Reception.

He hated crowded gatherings of that sort and seldom had any time for them; but Eloise Davenport liked to be escorted by a handsome man, and who could fill that position more appropriately than Rayburn Lyle?

She determined not only to look her best for him, but also to make sure that neither of them was overlooked by those of their social friends who were present at Roehampton House.

She was wearing a new gown which had just arrived from Paris of rose-pink silk ornamented with

innumerable frills round the hem. Her hat, covered in
roses and ostrich feathers, was a creation from which
no woman in the room could take her eyes.

The men, however, stared at Eloise Davenport's
lovely face, flashing dark eyes, and provocative
mouth, and told themselves that Rayburn Lyle was
damned lucky!

Viola gazed entranced.

She did not miss the manner in which having left
the Marchioness's side Lady Davenport turned to
look at Rayburn Lyle from under her eye-lashes and
her gloved hand rested for a moment on his arm.

Then, moving with the pride and elegance of a
swan floating over a silver lake, she swept into the
Reception-Room, the feathers of her exquisite hat and
the rose-pink frills of her gown floating behind her.

They seemed as she moved to draw attention to
the tininess of her pulled-in waist and the inviting
curve of her bosom, on which rested six strands of
huge pearls.

"She is lovely!" Viola told herself. "And of course
he must be in love with her."

She would have been extremely stupid if she had
not been aware that every beautiful married woman
in Society indulged in flirtations and *affaires de coeur*
which were like scalps hanging from the belt of a
Red Indian.

"I am very unfashionable, darling," she remembered hearing her mother say once to her father, "but
I have no wish to dance with anyone but you, and if
I have to flirt in a Conservatory there is no-one else
with whom I could feel the least flirtatious."

Her father had laughed and put his arm round her
mother's waist and pulled her close to him.

"And do you think I can see any other woman in
the room when you are present?" he enquired.

"I am often afraid that you might," her mother
answered in a low voice. "They are like lovely birds of
Paradise and I am sure that by comparison I am only
a little brown sparrow."

"There is no comparison," Sir Richard said firmly,

"and to me you are lovelier and more entrancing than any song-bird the world has ever known."

There had been a note in his voice which Viola, young though she was, had found very moving.

She had always remembered that interchange between her father and mother and told herself that that was what it meant to be in love! One day, she was sure, she would love a man in the same way and he would love her.

She saw several people speak to Rayburn Lyle and his smile flashed across his face in response to something they had said.

"He is very attractive," she told herself, and recalled how kind he had been to her.

She wondered if she could tell him that she had not encountered as much difficulty at home as she had anticipated.

Then she thought how bored he would be having to bother with her when he could talk to the alluring, exotic bird of Paradise with whom he had come to the Reception.

It was exactly the right description for Lady Davenport and Viola wished that her father was still alive so that she could ask him more about the beautiful women whom he had met at Buckingham Palace and whose pictures she had seen so often in the newspapers.

But after her mother, her father had admired more than anyone else the Queen, who had been the beautiful Danish-born Princess of Wales.

"She has a beauty which is difficult to describe," he said once, "and she makes every other woman in a Ball-Room fade into insignificance."

He had gone on to describe the Queen's tendency to be unpunctual, which infuriated the King, and her gaiety, which even when her deafness became more pronounced always seemed to make the dullest Court function amusing.

"I wonder what Papa would have thought of Lady Davenport," Viola found herself asking as she and her Stepmother drove back to Curzon Street.

Because she could not get those beautiful dark eyes out of her mind she asked tentatively:

"Do you know Lady Davenport, *Madre?*"

"I have met her," Lady Brandon replied. "A tiresome, frivolous woman, the typical feather-brained nit-wit that most men find entertaining."

"You sound as if you dislike her," Viola could not help saying.

"I dislike everything she stands for," Lady Brandon replied, "and I can assure you, Viola, she would not be the slightest help even if she wished to join us."

Viola was sure that that was the truth.

She could not imagine Lady Davenport shouting her protests in the street or being prepared to suffer for the Cause in which she believed.

She was also quite sure that Rayburn Lyle was not interested in the Suffragette Movement.

It was doubtful if he would even vote for the Bill which was shortly coming before Parliament and on which her Stepmother and her colleagues set so much store.

Viola felt too that he would have forgotten her from the moment he had sent her home in his brougham. If he did remember, it would be with irritation because the bomb must undoubtedly have damaged his carpet.

"All the same, I should so much like to talk to him again," she told herself, and she wished now that she had been brave enough to approach him at the Reception.

Rayburn Lyle had in fact been extremely bored.

He had been persuaded by Eloise Davenport into doing what he did not wish to do and he realised too late that he had made a mistake from his own point of view.

While he was prepared to philander, flirt, and enjoy the favours of any married woman he fancied, he had no desire to give rise to an open scandal.

For one thing, he disliked being gossipped about,

and secondly he had no intention of doing anything which might damage his career.

He enjoyed political life, but he was well aware that a politician was expected to be above suspicion, like "Caesar's wife," and Eloise Davenport was far too flamboyant and too unrestrained for their liaison to go unnoticed.

To have arrived together at the Marchioness of Roehampton's Reception was, Rayburn Lyle realised now, an error which could ignite a conflagration of gossip which would be hard to extinguish.

Leaving Eloise's side, he deliberately sought the company of elderly men and talked to them with a charm that never failed.

He found the Marquess of Londonderry deep in conversation with the Earl of Croxdale and they both seemed pleased to see him.

"I want to talk to you about Ireland," the Marquess said. "Come and dine with me one evening next week, Lyle, when you can get away from the House."

"I shall be delighted," Rayburn Lyle replied.

"I too have an invitation for you," the Earl of Croxdale said. "I am having a house-party in the country next weekend and I shall be disappointed if you refuse to be one of my guests."

"May I let you know in the morning?" Rayburn Lyle asked. "I have not my diary with me."

When he was driving Eloise Davenport back to her house in Belgrave Square she asked:

"What are you doing next weekend? George will still be away and I thought we might go to the country—together."

There was an obvious innuendo in her words and hastily Rayburn Lyle made up his mind to accept the Earl's invitation.

"I am sorry, Eloise," he replied, "but if you had let me know before I might have been able to arrange something. As it is, I have accepted another invitation. I thought your husband would have returned by then."

"So did I," Eloise Davenport agreed, "but I had a letter this morning saying that he thought it unlikely he could get back before the twentieth."

She gave a short laugh.

"George is enjoying himself in Paris. He always says that all his time is strictly spent on the race-course or with other owners, but I cannot help suspecting that it is more a case of *cherchez la femme!*"

Rayburn Lyle did not reply and after a moment she put her hand into his.

"It is a wonderful opportunity for us to be together," she said softly, "and various of my friends would be only too delighted to invite us to join their house-parties. I know that the Marlboroughs are entertaining."

"I am sorry, Eloise," Rayburn Lyle said again, "but this weekend is impossible."

He knew only too well how the great hostesses accommodated those who wished to be together.

The question of the arrangement of the bed-rooms always gave them cause for anxious thought. It was considered necessary to be helpful and at the same time discreet.

If, as Eloise had suggested, they should both accept an invitation to a country house, they would certainly be put in the same wing, although their bed-rooms would not be too obviously side by side.

It was all part of the enormous forethought that went into entertaining.

Weekend parties were, Rayburn Lyle sometimes thought, organised like military expeditions.

There was a continuous sequence of food and drink from eight o'clock in the morning to late at night, and the entertainments were as lavish as money and a superb organisation could make them.

In the winter there was hunting, shooting, and a new sport called golf, followed by Balls at night after huge dinner-parties of over fifty guests.

In the summer there would be cricket matches, boating, tennis, croquet, and garden-parties with the women all looking like full-blown peonies or many-petalled roses.

The stage would be set like a musical comedy, Rayburn Lyle often thought, and even the music was seldom lacking.

"Are you coming in with me now?" he heard Eloise ask, interrupting his train of thought.

"I am sorry. I must go to the House."

"You will be there until late?"

"I am afraid so."

"Then you will come to tea tomorrow?"

"I shall hope that nothing will prevent me."

"Time will pass very slowly," she said softly.

He looked down into her eyes and thought as he had often thought before that she was the most dramatically beautiful woman he had ever known.

He was also well aware of the smouldering fire that lingered in the depths of her dark eyes.

Passionately she was almost insatiable, and although he had told himself that he must be more circumspect, he was already beginning to regret that he had refused to accompany her to a weekend in the country.

'I can always change my mind,' he thought.

"I want to be with you," Eloise whispered as if she read his thoughts.

She lifted her lips to his, her dark eyes narrowing over a glint of fire.

Because he could not help himself he put his arms round her.

*   *   *

"The Earl of Croxdale has asked us both to stay with him next weekend," Lady Brandon said as the carriage carried her and Viola back to Curzon Street.

Aggressive and ultra-modern in other ways, she still preferred to drive about London behind two well-bred horses wearing tight bearing-reins.

To Viola also they meant far more than a motor-car, however smart and up-to-date it might be.

Her mother had been an outstanding horsewoman and Viola loved riding.

Horses meant more to her than friends, and one of the things she missed unbearably since her father's death was the ride she used to have with him every morning, whatever the weather and whatever the time of year.

In the country they would gallop wildly, to return to the house glowing with health and hungry for breakfast.

In London they rode sedately in the fashionable part of the Row and exercised their horses more energetically in the part where they were not overlooked.

Riding with a groom after her father's death could never mean the same to her and Lady Brandon was always too busy to ride.

"Shall I take a riding-habit with me to Croxdale Park?" Viola asked.

She had the idea that the Earl was a race-horse owner, in which case he was likely to have a number of excellent horses both to ride and to drive.

"I really ought not to spare the time to go gallivanting in the country," Lady Brandon said, "but Lord Croxdale was so insistent that we should be his guests. As he is enormously wealthy, I might persuade him to contribute a considerable sum to our funds."

"Surely it would not be right to ask for money if we are already his guests?" Viola questioned.

Whatever the cause, however deserving the charity, something within her shrank from begging for money especially from a new acquaintance.

But Lady Brandon had no such scruples.

"He will find it more difficult to refuse when I am his guest," she said. "Besides, there are sure to be other rich men there. They flock together like birds of the same feather."

"I would be quite happy to refuse the invitation," Viola said tentatively.

She was remembering the way the Earl had held her hand and she decided that she had no wish to see him again.

It would be nice to go to the country, to leave London and the interminable fear of becoming involved with the Police. At the same time . . .

Her thoughts shied away from what she half-suspected and yet was afraid to put into words.

Then she told herself she must have imagined that the Earl had any more interest in her than any elderly man might show to a very young girl.

'He is old enough to be my father,' she thought.

At the same time she knew she was only making excuses for something that her instinct told her was both wrong and unpleasant.

"We will go," Lady Brandon replied. "I am sure Lord Croxdale can be persuaded into giving me a cheque for a hundred pounds or perhaps more. Why not? It would mean nothing to him."

"I dare say he supports many more . . . urgent charities," Viola said unwisely.

"Urgent? What is more urgent than that women should be freed from their political shackles?" Lady Brandon asked sharply. "Can you still be so stupid as not to see that the appalling manner in which we are treated as a sex cannot be allowed to continue?"

She paused, then she said:

"You really should stop thinking about yourself, Viola—heaven knows, you have little enough cause—and consider the wretched women of all classes that we represent. They look to us to bring them out of the slough of despondency and into the light of emancipation."

Lady Brandon spoke with a fanatical note in her voice, but Viola thought that once again she was rehearsing some of the telling phrases she had used before and would use over and over again in her speeches.

The carriage drew up outside the house in Curzon Street and they both alighted.

As the Butler opened the front door he said:

"Miss Christabel Pankhurst is waiting to see you in the Drawing-Room, My Lady."

With an expression of pleasure on her face Lady Brandon hurried up the stairs, and because she knew it would be expected of her, Viola went too.

Actually she liked Christabel Pankhurst, whose

redoubtable mother led the women's fight for recognition.

Christabel had thrown herself heart and soul into the battle and had been to prison several times, charged with assaulting Policemen, hitting them in the mouth, and spitting in their faces.

She looked too pretty with her round face and laughing eyes to have a will of iron and the strength which carried her to the forefront of every demonstration.

"I am so glad to see you, Christabel!" Lady Brandon said, holding out both her hands, then kissing the girl on her cheek.

"Mother has sent me along with a lot of messages— Hello, Viola."

"Hello," Viola replied.

"I think we have discovered what happened to your bomb," Christabel said.

Viola drew in a deep breath.

"What have you discovered?" she asked nervously.

"One of our supporters is friendly with a kitchen-maid in Rayburn Lyle's household," Christabel replied. "We asked her to find out exactly what occurred."

Viola waited apprehensively.

"What were you told?" Lady Brandon asked.

"Well, according to the kitchen-maid, Rayburn Lyle rang the bell at about eight o'clock and told the men-servants to clear away a bomb which had not exploded but had made a mess on the hearth-rug in his Study."

"On the hearth-rug?" Lady Brandon ejaculated.

She turned to look at Viola accusingly.

"I told you to hide the bomb, you little idiot! Why did you deliberately disobey my instructions?"

The ferocity in her tone made Viola's voice die in her throat; her lips felt dry and it was almost impossible to answer.

"I suppose you lost your head," Lady Brandon went on, "and just put the bomb down on the floor and scuttled out of the house like a frightened rabbit."

"Well, anyway, it should have gone off wherever it was," Christabel interposed. "As far as we can ascertain, Mr. Lyle must have found it unexploded when he returned home."

She made an exasperated sound.

"That is the third bomb which has proved to be a dud! As I said to Mother, we shall really have to find someone more efficient to make them."

"I agree with you there," Lady Brandon said. "At the same time, that does not excuse Viola's behaviour."

"Oh, never mind," Christabel said good-humouredly. "We will give her a better job next time."

As if she could not bear any more, Viola turned and ran from the room. She went upstairs to her bed-room and taking off her hat sat down on the stool in front of the dressing-table.

It was typical, she thought, of her bad luck that the Pankhursts should have been able to find out where she had placed the bomb.

She knew how furious this would make her Stepmother, and she was quite certain that in consequence she would insist on her being given some other task which would involve even greater penalties.

She stared at her reflection in the mirror, seeing her eyes wide, dark, and frightened, and the pallor of her face.

She looked very lovely, although all she saw was in fact a foolish girl who could not fight against her Stepmother or even be astute enough to do anything correctly.

She felt the tears come into her eyes from sheer terror of what lay ahead.

She was quite sure that downstairs Lady Brandon was asking Christabel what action she could take to ensure the maximum amount of publicity.

"I cannot bear it," Viola moaned. "I cannot risk being successful next time and going to prison."

She sprang up and walked across the room to open a drawer where she had placed various newspaper reports concerning the Suffragettes.

She had kept them because they had frightened her and because she had tried to tell herself that it was wise to know what she must expect if found guilty of a crime.

She picked up one which, written by Mrs. Pankhurst, described what had happened to her the previous year.

I was found guilty and sentenced either to pay a fine of one pound, or undergo fourteen days for my sins in the third and lowest class. Of course I chose the latter alternative and was taken to join my comrades in the cells. Suppose yourself to be one of the third-class prisoners.

Every morning whilst it is still dark you will be awakened by the tramp of heavy feet and the ringing of bells. Then the light is turned on.

You wash in the tiny basin and dress hurriedly. Soon you hear the rattle of keys and noise of iron doors. The wardress flings yours open and orders sharply: "Empty your slops"

You hasten to do so and return at the word of command. You roll your bed, clean your tins. You have three pieces of rag with which to do this. Someone has left you a pail of water and you must scrub the stool, the bed, the table, wash the shelves, then scrub the floor.

Before you have done your task there comes again the jangling of keys and clanging of doors—"Where's your pint?"

You hand it out and it is filled with gruel, oatmeal, and water, without any seasoning, and six ounces of bread. It is thrust upon your plate.

You eat your breakfast and then begin to sew. Perhaps it is a sheet you have to do. The minimum quantity you must finish, as you will learn from your labour-card, is fifteen a week.

Can they really all be criminals, these poor, sad-faced women amongst you? Few seem young. All are anxious and careworn. They are broken down by poverty, sorrow, and overwork. How can these women bear the slow-going, long hours?

Viola read it through carefully.

She had read it often before, but each time it seemed more poignant, more frightening, because she knew that sooner or later it must happen to her.

Then with her hands trembling she picked up another statement that had been made by a Mrs. Mary Leigh.

She had been punished for breaking the windows of her cell. She had been stripped and handcuffed with her hands behind her during the day except at meals when the palms were placed together in front.

She had gone on hunger-strike and she wrote:

I was surrounded and forced back into a chair which was tilted backwards. There were about ten persons round me. The Doctor then forced my mouth so as to form a pouch and held me while one of the wardresses poured some liquid from a spoon. Saturday afternoon the wardresses forced me onto the bed and two Doctors came in with them.

While I was held down a nasal tube was inserted. It was two yards long with a funnel at the end and there is a glass in the middle to see if the liquid is passing. One end is put up the right and left nostril on alternate days.

Great pain is experienced during the process, both mental and physical. The drums of the ears seem to be bursting and there is a horrible pain in the throat and breast.

The after-effects are a feeling of faintness and a great pain in the nose and ears. I was very sick after the tube was withdrawn.

There was a great deal more in the statement, but Viola could not read it. Instead she put the cuttings back in the drawer.

She walked to the window to stare out with unseeing eyes at the sunshine on the grey roofs.

"I cannot . . . bear it! I cannot . . . bear it!" she whispered.

She heard the door of her bed-room open and turned her head.

Her Stepmother came into the room grim-faced and with a determined manner which made Viola feel her heart had stopped beating.

CHAPTER THREE

Rayburn Lyle looked at his watch and realised that he was likely to be late for a Committee in the House of Commons.

He had had to attend the Westminster Police Station, and this had disarranged his usual meticulous programme, in which he prided himself he was never late.

Ten days ago, as he had left the House of Commons by the St. Stephen's entrance, he had found himself in a seething crowd of people who were bringing a petition to the House and were endeavouring to force the Police into letting them into the lobbies.

The Police attempted to clear a passage for Rayburn Lyle so that he could reach his brougham.

But while they were doing so and he was finding it difficult to force a way through the crowd of men and women, most of whom were shouting at the tops of their voices, Rayburn Lyle had his pocket picked.

He did not particularly mind losing his wallet, which contained only a small sum of money, but the thief had also taken his gold cigar-case.

This he had been given by his father, Lord Walmsley, and it had in fact originally belonged to his grandfather.

Lord Walmsley was exceedingly sentimental about family possessions, especially those which had a history attached to them.

The cigar-case had been given to the Second Baron when he was a very young man by the famous Duke of Wellington.

He had treasured it all his life and passed it on to his son, the present Lord Walmsley, who in actual fact did not smoke cigars.

"I hope you will find this useful, my boy," Rayburn's father had said to him, "and do not lose it. I consider it an heirloom, which one day you will pass on to your son."

Rayburn Lyle was not a heavy smoker, but he enjoyed a good cigar after luncheon and dinner, and because he knew it would please his father, he carried them in the gold cigar-case.

It was therefore extremely annoying that it should have been stolen, and he knew that when he had to confess that he had lost the case, Lord Walmsley would be upset.

Rayburn Lyle had every reason to be grateful to his father.

Lord Walmsley had decided five years ago that he wished to retire to Scotland to spend what remained of his life salmon-fishing.

He owned a large Estate with a magnificent Castle on the bank of the Spey, and although at one time he had been the Liberal Spokesman in the House of Lords, he was content now to leave all political ambitions to his son.

He therefore had made over to Rayburn the Walmsley Estates in Hampshire and a very large fortune.

Because he was devoted to his father, Rayburn was determined that he should never feel that his trust had been misplaced.

In fact, he administered the Estates admirably and had received an enthusiastic letter of congratulation from Lord Walmsley when he had been appointed Under-Secretary of State for Foreign Affairs.

At the same time, he thought with a wry smile, nothing would irritate his father more than to learn that he had lost the cigar-case, which had been presented to his grandfather by the Iron Duke.

He had informed the Police of the theft without much hope of recovery.

They in their turn had notified all the known "fences" in London and publicised as much as possible the large reward which Rayburn Lyle offered for the return of his prized possession.

He was therefore delighted when early this morning a Policeman had knocked at the door of his house in Queen Anne's Gate to tell him that a cigar-case answering the description of the one he had lost was waiting for identification at Westminster Police Station.

Having thanked the Constable, Rayburn Lyle finished his breakfast and entering his electric brougham told the chauffeur to hurry.

The traffic, however, delayed them longer than he expected, and when finally they drew up outside the austere building Rayburn Lyle hurried quickly inside and informed the Sergeant at the desk why he had come.

He was ushered to a room where the Officer in charge of the Station was waiting for him with not only his cigar-case but also his wallet.

Needless to say, the money had gone but the thief had obviously found it difficult to get rid of the Moroccan-leather case with gold corners and Rayburn Lyle's monogram embossed in the centre of it.

For the cigar-case, he learnt, the thief had received the meagre sum of three pounds from a "fence" in the East End who knew it would be a difficult object to sell again.

Rayburn Lyle paid all the dues and put the cigar-case back in his pocket.

"It's rather a valuable object to carry about, Sir," the Police Officer said respectfully. "London is full of pick-pockets at this time of the year, and demonstrations outside the House of Commons make an easy picking-ground."

"I will be more careful in future," Rayburn Lyle promised with a smile. "I am extremely grateful to you, Officer."

"We're not always so lucky! Will you please sign here?"

Rayburn Lyle wrote his signature where it was required. Then holding out his hand he said:

"I hope I shall not have to trouble your you again, but thank you once more."

"I'll see you to the door, Sir," the Police Officer replied.

They stepped out into the passage and as they did so a number of women escorted by Policemen were being led through a door which Rayburn Lyle knew led into the Magistrates' Court.

"Suffragettes!" the Police Officer explained before he could ask the obvious question. "They'll get short shrift today from Mr. Curtis-Bennett. He feels violently against Women's Suffrage."

"They are certainly gluttons for punishment," Rayburn Lyle murmured.

"That's true enough," the Police Officer answered, "and this lot deliberately caused a riot in Downing Street and would have stormed Number 10 if my men hadn't prevented it."

Rayburn Lyle did not answer.

At that moment, walking last in the procession of women, each escorted by two Policemen, he had seen Viola!

* * *

As Lady Brandon entered the bed-room Viola had known what she might expect from her Stepmother and braced herself to endure physical pain.

She was not mistaken.

Lady Brandon walked across the room and slapped her first on one side of her face, then on the other.

"You little liar!" she said viciously. "You told me you had hidden the bomb, but you did nothing of the sort!"

The impact of her hands was extremely painful, but Viola's pride did not let her wince away or even cry out.

She just stood facing her Stepmother, her cheeks beginning to burn from the blows, but her eyes were quite steady.

"You have let me down in front of my friends," Lady Brandon stormed. "I am ashamed of you—bitterly and deeply ashamed!"

There was no doubt that she felt personally outraged, and since in some ways Viola could understand what her Stepmother was feeling she managed to say in a low voice:

"I am ... sorry, *Madre*."

"I cannot understand, when I can convert so many other women to a sense of their responsibilities, that I should be such an abject failure where you are concerned," Lady Brandon said bitterly.

She looked at Viola contemptuously and went on:

"Change your clothes. I am going to make you see what our supporters will endure for their faith and their ideals, and perhaps you will begin to understand how heroic they are in facing martyrdom for the cause of freedom."

"Change my ... clothes?" Viola asked. "Where are we ... going?"

"You will see," Lady Brandon answered. "Put on something plain. We are only to be spectators, not demonstrators."

She went from the room and because Viola had no choice she changed into a gown of pale lilac ornamented with nothing more elaborate than a small lace collar.

It had a belt of deep purple satin which fastened round her small waist and her purple hat which was brimless was trimmed merely with ribbons of the same colour.

Viola felt apprehensive as to where her Stepmother was taking her, but she was aware that a deputation of Suffragettes or a demonstration had lately been restricted to no more than thirteen individuals.

This was a device used by the Women's Suffrage Movement to avoid breaking the law that prohibited large assemblies within a one-mile radius of the House of Commons.

Deputations of thirteen could therefore approach the House without disobeying Police regulations.

When Viola was ready she went downstairs to the Hall to find that her Stepmother was already waiting for her.

She carried a box of leaflets and handed another box to Viola.

"Carry these," she said. "I suppose you can distribute them without making a mistake or dropping them down a drain! Heaven knows it is impossible to make you do anything properly!"

Without waiting for a reply she led the way through the front door to where the carriage was waiting.

Viola followed her Stepmother and when the horses had set off down Curzon Street she asked in a low voice:

"Where are we going?"

"Christabel tells me that a deputation of women is carrying a petition to Number 10 Downing Street this evening. It is known that the Prime Minister has called a Cabinet Meeting for six-thirty P.M., and the Ministers will enter the meeting with the cry of "Votes for Women" ringing in their ears."

"Surely no-one will be allowed to cause a . . . disturbance in . . . Downing Street?" Viola asked hesitatingly.

"If we make up our minds to cause a disturbance, we cause one!" Lady Brandon replied positively. "There is always a crowd outside Number 10, and all you have to do, Viola, is to hand out your leaflets. Do you understand?"

"Yes, *Madre*," Viola answered meekly.

She felt sure there would be difficulties ahead, but it was a relief to know that she had to do nothing more aggressive than give away pieces of paper.

She glanced into the open box and saw with consternation that the leaflets were inflammatory, calling on women to defy the Government, to use every method in their power to be obstructive and demand the vote.

They drove on, and when they reached Whitehall, Lady Brandon stopped the carriage a little distance away from the turning into Downing Street.

"Wait here," she told the coachman.

It was a comfort for Viola to know that she intended to return home and they would therefore not be embroiled in arrests which she was certain would take place.

When they entered the street, it was to find the usual crowd of sight-seers outside Number 10, but for the moment there was no sign of any disturbance.

Lady Brandon walked briskly along the left-hand side of the street until keeping well behind the sight-seers they were almost opposite the famous door with its polished brass number and gleaming knocker.

There was a Policeman standing on either side of it and other Police lined up along the railings facing the crowd.

They were obviously anticipating trouble, Viola thought. Then, as an electric brougham carrying a Member of the Cabinet turned into the street, the noise began.

Women seemed to appear from nowhere, and pulling back the thin coats they wore over their dresses they revealed the slogan *Votes for Women* emblazoned across their chests.

They rushed into the centre of the road, shouting and screaming.

They seemed to take the Police by surprise and the Constables stepped hurriedly forward, but not before one of the women had smashed a window of the electric brougham with the handle of her sun-shade.

She was seized by two Policemen, but the crowd surging forward to get a good view of what was occurring gave another woman time to rush onto the steps of Number 10 and scatter a cloud of leaflets.

The Cabinet Minister rushed hastily into the house, but already his hat had been knocked off and he had received several blows on his back.

More Police came running down the street and now the women, still shouting and screaming their protests, were firmly held by both arms in a manner which made it impossible for them to do any more damage.

Other Police were pushing the crowd back and in a few seconds it appeared that they had the situation under control.

It was then, as Viola stood watching what was happening and holding her box of leaflets in her arms, that she received a powerful push in her back between her shoulder-blades.

It was so violent that it sent her sprawling forward through a gap between the people in front of her and she was only prevented from falling to the ground because she came into collision with a Policeman.

Putting out her hands to regain her balance, she held on to him, and her box of leaflets falling to the ground was scattered in the street.

He caught hold of her arm and two seconds later, without a word being spoken, she found herself being marched by two Policemen in the wake of the other women who were already being moved down the street.

"No, no! I am not with them ... !" she began.

Then she realised that the spilled leaflets were evidence that could not be explained away.

The words died on her lips and she knew as she was dragged relentlessly forward who had pushed her and who was responsible for her arrest.

She did not even need to look back to know that there would be a look of triumph on her Stepmother's face.

A Black Maria was waiting at the end of Downing Street and as the Suffragettes were piled into it they started laughing and congratulating themselves on being so successful.

"I had no idea we would get so near to Number 10," a lady who was sitting next to Viola said.

She had a cultured voice and was in fact extremely attractive. Her clothes were expensive and

the lady who answered her from the other side of
the Black Maria was equally well dressed and obviously well bred.

"I told the Prime Minister a month ago at a dinner-party that we should be bearding him in Downing
Street before we finished."

Several women who were listening laughed.

"I wish we had the chance to break the windows
of *his* carriage."

"We will do so sooner or later! If only Herbert
Asquith had been the first to arrive! He deserves all
the blows we can inflict on him."

"They should all be shot!" the lady who was sitting next to Viola exclaimed. "Sooner or later they will
have to listen to us, even though it will go against the
grain."

"It will certainly do that," someone laughed.
"What man ever wants to listen to a woman unless she
is flattering him?"

"That is one thing I have vowed never to do
again," a rather sprightly blonde remarked. "I think
all men are beasts and the sooner they hear us say so
the better!"

There was something spiteful in the speaker's
voice. Then the lady sitting opposite said to Viola:

"I have not seen you before. What is your name?"

"Viola Brandon."

"Oh, of course. You are Mavis's stepdaughter.
She has talked about you. Well, we are very pleased
to welcome you as a fellow-martyr."

Viola longed to say that she had no wish to be a
martyr but knew that they would not understand,
and anything she might say to excuse herself would
in fact be unfair to her Stepmother.

The ladies were all very pleased with themselves.

Viola could not help thinking they exuded the
same satisfaction as naughty children who had raided
an orchard or were enjoying a midnight feast that
was not permitted by their teacher.

It was not a long way to Westminster Police

Station, and as they entered, being hurried up the steps in case their appearance excited the interest of the passers-by, Viola felt as if all the warmth had left her body.

She knew it was fear and told herself she should be ashamed of being so frightened when her companions were so unconcerned at the thought of what awaited them.

It was in the Police Station that Viola realised for the first time that it was not really a deputation in which she was involved, and that twenty women had been arrested including herself.

"Only twenty of us?" one Suffragette said in disgust. "There should be many more! Last week they arrested fifty-seven, but then Christabel Pankhurst was arranging it."

Viola said nothing. She could not help hoping, because there were so few of them, that the Magistrate would not take such a serious view of the disturbance.

She was however not very optimistic.

As it was late at night they were told that they would spend the night in the cells and be tried in the morning.

The cells had little or no comfort and were large enough for ten of their number to be locked in one and ten in another.

It was a crush and there was no question of their lying down or even being able to rest.

There were only hard benches round the walls on which they could sit, but the ladies settled themselves as if they were the softest sofas or arm-chairs in their luxurious Mansions.

One lady had brought some peppermints with her, which she passed round, and another had a tiny phial of perfume with which to scent her handkerchief, and she suggested to her friends that they do the same.

"It is the smell of this place that I cannot stand," she exclaimed.

Viola agreed with her.

There was a dank, damp stink of cold stones and unwashed bodies that she thought was repugnant.

The floor was clean, but the barred window high up at the top of the cell was dirty and let in very little of the evening light.

Because she did not know what to expect she said to the lady sitting next to her:

"Do we stay . . . here all . . . night?"

"Of course," was the reply. "And I hope you had a substantial meal to eat before you came out. His Majesty does not offer us food or drink until we reach Holloway and then we refuse his hospitality!"

Viola remembered the small iced cakes and the sandwich she had eaten at the Marchioness of Roehampton's reception and thought that that could hardly be described as a substantial meal.

She was not in the least hungry but she felt thirsty, and knew it was due partly to fear and partly to the airless, dry atmosphere of the cell and the fact that it was packed with so many people.

But she told herself she was fortunate to be with ladies of her own class rather than drunken tramps or women who had been brought in off the streets.

"As long as we are here," someone said, "we might as well make a nuisance of ourselves. Let us start by telling them what we want and what eventually they will have to give us."

There was laughter and then their voices all screamed out: "Votes for Women!" "Down with the Government!" "Votes for Women!" until the walls of the cell seemed to ring with the noise.

Viola thought she ought to join in but her voice felt as if it was strangled in her throat.

She could not help wondering whether, if they were given the vote, these women would be satisfied, or whether in fact their campaigning, whatever the result, was a delight in itself.

As the hours of the night went slowly by she felt that that was in fact the truth.

When they were not shouting they were giggling and gossiping amongst themselves, criticising their leaders and the way in which the campaigns and the meetings were being conducted.

They also talked boastfully of what they intended to do in the future.

"I said to Sylvia Pankhurst the sooner we plant a bomb in the Chamber of the House of Commons, the better!" one lady said.

"You will find it difficult to carry it in," another remarked. "Already they are suspicious of large muffs, and I am told that a woman has to open her handbag."

"That is an outrage in itself!" someone cried. "A man does not have to carry a bag, so it is unfair that we should be suspected because it is part of our usual attire."

"Mrs. Pankhurst has asked for ideas," a pretty brunette remarked, "and I have quite a number that I intend to put before the next Executive Meeting."

"We must get the support of Lady Henry Somerset," the lady next to Viola said. "She and Mrs. Alfred Lyttleton can gain us far more publicity than most of us can."

"Well, personally, I pin my faith on seeing Lady Frances Balfour in the headlines," the brunette remarked. "Think what it means to have a name like that at the top of our list."

"More and more people are beginning to realise that what we are claiming is right," a lady next to Viola replied, "and it is only a question of time before the whole world acknowledges us."

Viola could not help feeling that this was optimistic, but there was a murmur of approval from the other women listening and she knew she was very much in the minority.

To pass away the time they sang hymns and many of the songs from the musical comedies.

These made Viola remember that she had accepted the invitation from Lord Croxdale to be at the opening night of *The Merry Widow*.

People had already been talking about it and she was looking forward to seeing the show even though she felt uncomfortable at the idea of the Earl being her host.

'I am being stupid,' she thought. 'But anyway now I cannot go to the theatre with him, and after my name appears in the newspapers he will probably not wish to know me.'

The Earl was a friend of the King, and His Majesty was known to be against Women's Suffrage.

'I am sure Papa would have been too,' she decided.

She wondered what he would say if he could have seen her at the moment shut up in a cell and facing imprisonment.

She considered how long the sentence would be. Long enough, she supposed, to ensure that not only could she not go to the theatre, but neither could she visit the Earl's house in the country at the weekend.

She questioned if her Stepmother would go to the house-party without her. She had a feeling that if she did, Lord Croxdale would be disappointed.

"Perhaps that will be a good thing," Viola told herself philosophically.

She remembered the uncomfortable sensations he had evoked in her and how she had felt frightened because his face was so near to hers.

"I was just being foolish," she told herself, and yet inescapably the feeling was still there—a feeling of positive revulsion.

Her thoughts went to Rayburn Lyle.

Would he be sorry when he heard that she was in prison? He had known how frightened she was at the thought of it.

He had been kind . . . very kind . . . not to have sent for the Police after finding the bomb in his Study.

She suddenly thought how horrifying it would have been if it had gone off as had been intended and not only wrecked his house but also maimed or perhaps killed him.

He had certainly been brave when he saw what was happening.

Another man might have hurriedly shut the door

and left her to her fate, but his first thought had been for her, to drag her behind the sofa and throw himself on top of her.

"I should have thanked him for that," Viola told herself.

She recalled how heavy his body had been as it covered hers, and yet frightened though she was, he had given her a sense of protection.

She had not felt revolted or disgusted by him.

The Earl had only touched her hand, and yet she had instinctively longed to snatch it away and at the same time felt herself shrink back in an effort to avoid him.

Why should there be such a difference between the two men?

Viola saw again Rayburn Lyle's handsome face and at the same time the expression in Lady Davenport's eyes as she looked up at him.

'She is very beautiful,' Viola thought, 'and he must love her . . . very much.'

The night seemed interminable and once or twice she found her head nodding, only to be awakened as her companions' cry rang out, "Votes for Women!" or they burst into song.

Finally a pale grey light came from above their heads and it was dawn.

They tidied themselves as best they could, borrowing a mirror from one lady, a comb from another.

Then several hours later the keys clanked in the lock of the cell, a row of Policemen appeared, and one by one they were taken outside.

"If it is Mr. Curtis-Bennett, expect the worst!" Viola heard one of the ladies say.

"See you in prison!" they cried cheerily to one another, and filed out with their heads held high, a look of defiance on their faces.

'They are brave, and really rather magnificent!' Viola thought.

She tried to walk proudly, at the same time aware that she had a feeling like a heavy stone within her breast, and despite every resolution her fingers were cold and trembling.

As the women disappeared inside the Police Court, Rayburn Lyle turned to the Officer standing beside him.

"May I speak to the lady who went last in the procession?"

The Police Officer shook his head.

"I'm afraid not, Sir, but I can speak to her if you would like to give me a message."

"I do wish her to have one," Rayburn Lyle said.

He drew the Officer to one side and spoke to him in a low voice. He then walked quickly out of the Police Station and got into his brougham, which was waiting outside.

The Police Officer went into the Court.

It was packed with a large number of the Press, as was usual on these occasions, and they were already scribbling away in their note-books.

The public seats were filled too, the majority being spectators who were there to watch a bit of fun, some of them getting a vicarious amusement out of seeing Ladies of Quality "making fools of themselves."

The others were poor women who felt that there must be something in a cause which commanded the attention of their betters.

Mr. Curtis-Bennett was sharp and business-like.

The women who had been arrested were, Viola learnt, led by a Mrs. Despard, who was well known as one of the leaders of the Movement.

She had been in the other cell all night and had obviously rehearsed what she intended to say. She now started to explain to the Magistrate that their protest was the beginning of a campaign which would not cease until the Government yielded to women's demand for the vote.

"There can be no going back for us," she declared, "and more will happen if we do not get justice."

Mr. Curtis-Bennett rebuked her severely, saying

that these disgraceful scenes in the street must cease and the sooner they realised it the better.

"Twenty shillings or fourteen days!" he said sharply, and Mrs. Despard retorted proudly:

"I will go to prison because I am fighting for my rights."

The same alternative was put to the next woman in the dock and her answer was the same.

It was then that Viola, who was waiting at the end of the queue, found a Police Officer beside her.

He bent down and whispered in her ear:

"When you are given the same choice, Miss, pretend to collapse in a faint. Your fine will be paid and there is a gentleman waiting for you outside."

Viola's eyes widened and she looked at him in surprise. But before she could answer or question him in any way, he moved away and she heard another lady say:

"I will go to prison—and I curse the Government for its cruelty!"

Slowly the queue of women diminished as those who had already been charged were taken away to the cells and finally Viola was left alone in the dock.

She faced the Magistrate, feeling that her heart was beating loudly in her breast, at the same time trying to make up her mind what she should do.

She knew what was expected of her, knew what her Stepmother had intended when she had contrived her arrest.

She told herself she was a coward not to go through with it. At the same time, it was not her battle.

She was not really convinced in her heart that what these women demanded was right, and, even if it was, their methods were not those of which her father would have approved.

'There must be other ways!' she thought despairingly.

Even while she was still undecided, still wondering whether she should follow those who had preceded her to prison, she heard her name and the Magistrate say in a bored tone:

"Viola Brandon, you stand accused of the same offence—twenty shillings or fourteen days!"

It was perhaps the indifferent way he spoke without even looking at her which made Viola make up her mind.

It seemed so hopeless to pit one's wits against a man who was not even moved by such antagonism but merely thought that the whole proceeding was a nuisance.

She shut her eyes and because she was indeed feeling weak and very frightened it was quite easy to collapse on the floor.

She was lifted up somewhat roughly by two Police Constables and Viola felt herself being carried out of the Court.

As she did so she heard a man say:

"I have the money here, Your Worship, to pay this lady's fine."

"Next case!" Mr. Curtis-Bennett said sharply, and before Viola had left the Court another prisoner had shuffled into the dock.

She felt the fresh air on her face and knew she was being carried outside. Then she was lifted into a brougham, and as she was placed against the cushions she heard Rayburn Lyle's voice.

"Thank you, Constable."

The door was closed and the brougham drove off.

Viola opened her eyes and saw Rayburn Lyle smiling at her.

"You are a better actress than I gave you credit for," he said with a hint of laughter in his voice.

She sat up and straightened her hat.

"I . . . thought it must be . . . you who . . . saved me.

"Who else might have done so?" he enquired.

"No-one," she replied. "But how did you know I was there? How could you have known?"

"I happened by a lucky chance to be in the Police Station."

He saw the question in her eyes and laughed.

"No, I had not been arrested. I was merely there to collect something which had been stolen from me and which fortunately the Police were able to recover."

"And you saw . . . me?" Viola asked in a low voice.

"I saw you and realised that something very strange must have happened," he answered. "Or had you been planting another bomb?"

"No . . . nothing like that," Viola answered. "My Stepmother took me to watch a . . . demonstration outside Number 10 Downing Street, then . . ."

She paused.

She felt embarrassed at the thought of telling anyone of the way in which her Stepmother had treated her.

"What happened?" Rayburn Lyle prompted.

"Someone . . . it may have been . . . someone in the crowd," Viola said hastily, "pushed me against a . . . Constable . . . and the leaflets I was carrying in a box were spilled at his . . . feet."

She felt, although he did not say so, that Rayburn Lyle guessed who had pushed her.

"I warned you to take more care of yourself," he said.

"I tried to," she answered.

She drew in her breath.

"I think now I . . . hate the idea of having the . . . vote. . . . I do not . . . want one."

"I can understand that," he said, "and anyway you ought not to be worrying your head at your age about a vote, or politics at all, for that matter. You should be enjoying yourself as I am sure your father would have wished you to do were he alive."

"I would like to help some of the women who are suffering in the East End," Viola said. "I have read the Parliamentary reports on housing, lack of education, and the terrible poverty that exists in some parts of England. Would a vote for women solve any of them?"

"I feel quite certain it would not!" Rayburn Lyle answered. "You are quite right, Viola: women should concern themselves with helping the poor, the destitute, and not antagonise every man by making clowns of themselves."

He looked at her as he spoke, then went on in a different tone of voice:

"You are tired out. I suppose you had no sleep last night and I expect too you are hungry. Go home to bed and forget everything that has happened. It has been a horrible experience, but try not to let it occur again."

"I will . . . try," Viola said with a little catch in her voice.

She thought apprehensively that her Stepmother would be waiting for her at home.

In the night she had felt her cheeks still smarting from the blows she had received, but even so she was thankful that she had not been forced to suffer an even more violent punishment at Lady Brandon's hands.

What would she do now?

Involuntarily Viola shivered and Rayburn Lyle put out his hand to cover hers.

"Sooner or later," he said quietly, as if he knew what she was thinking, "you will have to be brave enough to refuse to take part in any more of these demonstrations. They always end up the same way."

When he touched her hand Viola unexpectedly felt a shiver that had run through her body turn to a warmth that was very different from anything she had ever felt before.

It seemed to be as much in her mind as in her body.

"When I am . . . with you," she said, "I feel brave . . . but when I am with . . . other people I am only conscious of being a . . . coward."

"I believe you are braver than you think you are," Rayburn replied. "When you are feeling better we must find a way to have a talk and try to find a solution to your problems."

"Could we do that?" Viola enquired.

"Why not?" he asked. "I spend a great deal of my life sorting out the difficulties of my Constituents, and I think if it comes to that you have a prior claim."

"If I . . . could talk to you . . . I would feel . . . much braver."

"We will arrange something for next week, if you promise in the meantime you will not get yourself involved in any more reprehensible actions so that you are detained at His Majesty's pleasure!"

"I will be very careful," Viola promised.

The brougham came to a standstill and she glanced out the window to see that they were at the bottom of Curzon Street where the chauffeur had stopped the previous time he had taken her home.

"You have been . . . very kind," she said. "More kind than I can possibly say. I am . . . deeply grateful."

"Then show your gratitude by keeping out of trouble," Rayburn Lyle admonished. "We will meet next week. In the meantime take care of yourself."

"Thank you again," she said in a low voice. "You have been . . . wonderful."

She looked into his eyes and for a moment both of them were very still.

Something strange seemed to pass between them, something which made Viola feel as if the electric brougham was filled with sunshine.

Then with a smile, almost as if he mocked himself, Rayburn lifted her hand and kissed it.

"Be a good girl," he said.

As she turned her face away from him towards the door, the chauffeur opened it and she stepped out onto the pavement.

Rayburn Lyle made no attempt to join her and she knew it was because he was aware that he should not be seen with her.

Nevertheless, as the brougham drove away and

she walked slowly up Curzon Street, she felt lonely and helpless because he was no longer beside her.

"He does make me feel brave," she told herself. "He gives me the courage I ought to have if I was not so foolish and fearful."

A servant let her into the house and as she stepped into the Hall Viola asked nervously:

"Is Her Ladyship at home?"

"No, Miss Viola. Her Ladyship went out early this morning and said she would not be back until tea-time."

Viola heaved a sigh of relief and ran upstairs.

As she had neared the house she had been terrified of enduring her Stepmother's interrogation and having to admit that while everyone else had gone to prison she had escaped.

She was well aware what Lady Brandon would think, even if she accepted the fact that she had fainted and had been unable to reply to the Magistrate.

She knew however there would be no reason for her Stepmother to suspect that anyone in particular would pay the fine.

There were always people in the Court philanthropic enough to offer to pay the fines of the Suffragettes, although their generosity was invariably refused.

But they still went on trying because to the general public the idea of a lady willingly subjecting herself to the indignities of Holloway was intolerable.

Upstairs Viola had a bath and got into bed. Then because the long night had been even more exhausting than she realised she fell into a deep, dreamless sleep.

She slept until late in the afternoon, then awoke to realise that she was ravenously hungry.

She rang the bell and a quarter of an hour later had just finished eating an omelette and was drinking a cup of tea when her Stepmother came into her bed-room.

Viola stiffened and her eyes were very dark and apprehensive as she waited for the storm to break over her head.

"What are you doing here?" Lady Brandon asked in a thunderous tone.

* * *

Seated in one of the decorative boxes at Daly's Theatre and waiting for the curtain to rise, Viola told herself that she should in fact be very grateful to the Earl of Croxdale.

It was entirely due to his invitation that Lady Brandon had restained her anger and that physically Viola had escaped unscathed.

There was no doubt that her Stepmother was contemptuous and bitter, and she used every term of abuse in her vocabulary to inform Viola how feeble, half-witted, and gutless she was.

But surprisingly she had believed that Viola really had fainted and had actually ceased abusing her simply because she wished to give her plenty of time in which to dress for the theatre.

"Lord Croxdale was very insistent that we should accompany him this evening," she said, "and although I hope you will feel ashamed as you think of those heroic women suffering in prison, we will join the Earl as arranged."

It was a relief to know that she had not to remain at home listening to her Stepmother's abuse.

It made Viola get dressed hastily and take pains to make herself look as attractive as possible.

Her gown was very glamorous.

Although she disliked her stepdaughter and privately humiliated her on every available occasion, Lady Brandon was not mean where Viola's clothes were concerned.

Indeed everything she put on became her, and her figure, if a little thin, was perfect. But her white gown had been expensive and the wrap that she draped over her shoulders was edged with swans'-down.

It gave her an ethereal look which made her outstanding even in a theatre filled with the cream of Society and amongst whom were all the acknowledged beauties of the year.

Glittering with jewels, their shoulders dazzlingly white against the black evening-suits of their escorts, they were, Viola thought, looking down into the stalls, as her mother had described to her—"glittering birds of Paradise."

Although she had often been to the theatre Viola had never before been in one of the large and important boxes.

She was well aware that a number of people in the audience were looking up curiously to see who was with the well-known Earl of Croxdale.

A first night was always fascinating and exciting.

There was a murmur of excitement from the audience that was like the buzzing of a swarm of bees and there was the magic of an indescribable, almost breathless anticipation.

The people in the pit were ready to jump to their feet and applaud any celebrity whom they recognised, and because it was an opening night, the majority of the theatre-going public in the more expensive seats were on time.

Watching them, Viola thought that nothing could equal the elegance of the men in their long-tailed coats, high collars, and white ties.

Even though she felt an inexplicable dislike for the Earl of Croxdale, she had to admit that when she arrived at his house it had been difficult not to admire him in his evening-clothes.

He had arranged with her Stepmother that they should have a light meal before they left for the theatre, then they would have supper afterwards.

The dinner he provided for them was not only delicious, it was also far more luxurious than anything Viola had enjoyed before.

There was caviar to start with and ortolans to follow, which had become fashionable because the King liked them, and as they were very small game birds from Europe, they were extremely expensive.

These dishes were followed by large hot-house peaches from the Earl's garden at Croxdale Park, cooked in brandy and brought flaming to the table.

The Earl and Lady Brandon drank champagne, as did their fourth guest, an elderly Peer who devoted himself exclusively to her Stepmother, leaving the Earl free to talk to Viola.

She could not help feeling that this had been carefully arranged by the Earl, especially when in the box at the theatre she found herself sitting next to him while her Stepmother was in the other corner of the box and divided from her by the Peer.

She looked at the audience, but was well aware as she did so that the Earl was watching her.

Nevertheless, when the curtain rose she forgot him in the excitement of listening to Lehar's exquisite music and watching the brilliance and colour of the opening chorus.

The Earl had told them at dinner how much depended on the success of tonight's performance.

George Edwardes, who was always known as "The Guv-nor" in the theatre-world, was in a bad way financially.

His luck was out, something seemed to have spoilt his fantastic flair for choosing shows that were winners.

While George Edwardes always seemed to know the public taste, the runs had been shorter, the takings poorer, the expenses higher, and yet his inevitable flair had told him that a change was wanted, and out of nowhere, as it seemed to the theatre-going world later, he produced Franz Lehar.

"Edwardes has given the lead to Lily Elsie," the Earl said at dinner. "You must have heard of her, Shandown, a pretty woman, not a great deal of voice."

"A very pretty woman!" the elderly Peer had agreed positively.

Viola had never seen Lily Elsie before, but her loveliness, her sophistication, and above all her glamour had not only captivated her by the end of the show but everyone else in the audience as well.

The singing seemed to be inspired, but perhaps more than the brilliance of the comics or the genius of George Graves there was the wonderful, unforgettable, haunting Viennese music which was being sung and whistled in the streets before the performance had ended.

"It was wonderful! Lovely! I have never seen anything so exciting!" Viola said enthusiastically, clapping her hands until they hurt.

"And you are lovely too!" the Earl said.

She came back from the dreamland to which *The Merry Widow* had taken her to be conscious that like a dark shadow his personality had been encroaching on her all through the performance.

She had been aware of him even while she tried not to be, and now, as she rose to her feet and he put her swans'-down-trimmed wrap round her shoulders, the touch of his fingers against her bare skin aroused in her a feeling of revulsion.

She wished that they did not have to go out to supper, then told herself severely that she was being very ungrateful.

The women she had been with last night were at this moment suffering the pangs of hunger in the darkness, desolation, and discomfort of Holloway.

She should really be with them, so how could she complain about anything, even the Earl of Croxdale, when she was free?

Because she was ashamed of her feelings she forced herself to smile at him and say:

"Thank you so much for bringing me here tonight. I shall always be grateful to you for an unforgettable experience."

"I want you to be grateful to me, Viola," he said, and his eyes were on her lips as he spoke.

CHAPTER FOUR

Rayburn Lyle walked across the Drawing-Room
to stand looking into the mirror over the mantelshelf
and adjusting his grey cravat.

If there was one thing which was really uncomfortable, he thought, it was making love in a
Drawing-Room.

But tea-time had become a time for romance and
it was quite usual for a gentleman to be asked to tea
alone by a lady who fancied him.

It was a fashion that had been set by King
Edward when he was Prince of Wales, who found
that the only time when he could escape from Marlborough House and his many commitments to call on
the lady of his choice was at four-thirty P.M.

Husbands were expected to go out to tea with
other men's wives if they were not at their Club.

Etiquette demanded that a gentleman who was
calling on a lady should never leave his top-hat,
gloves, or stick in the Hall, but lay them on the Drawing-Room floor as if he were just ready to depart.

The tea invitation could with care be reduced to
one caller, and servants were trained not to enter
the Drawing-Room unless the bell had rung for them.

Big sofas were as comfortable as feather-beds,
but nevertheless it required a great deal of persistence
and ingenuity to make love to a lady clothed in the
elaborate *toilette* which was worn in the afternoon.

It was in fact extremely difficult to seduce a
woman encased in a tight-laced corset which reached
from her bust to her hips.

She also probably wore little padded cushions to accentuate her behind, and a number of unfortunate females also padded their bosoms.

An inordinate amount of petticoats, long trailing skirts, frilled, ruched, and be-laced, presented an awkward obstacle at one end of the body, while a boned neck to the gown, even if it was of transparent lace, was fastened with innumerable small buttons down the back.

A woman might be a temptress, and undoubtedly was, but a man required not only great persistence and determination but also the dexterity of a lady's-maid if he desired to uncover and touch any part of her exquisitely curved body.

But then in the early years of the new century a genius called Lucille, who was in fact a lady by birth and the first to go into trade, invented the "tea-gown."

Nothing could have been more attractive or indeed more suitable for the intimate, romantic, and titillating seances that took place at tea-time.

Made of trailing chiffon, velvet, or silk, it fell from the lady's shoulders to the floor, making her look ethereal and at the same time provocative, while dispensing for that golden hour with the armoured corset.

Queen Alexandra set the seal of approval on the tea-gown when she presided over the tea-table in one of white silk covered with lace and worn with the most splendid jewels.

When Rayburn Lyle had entered Eloise Davenport's Drawing-Room that afternoon she had been waiting for him as he expected, wearing a tea-gown of green chiffon which revealed rather than concealed the exotic perfection of her sensuous body.

He put his tall hat, stick, and gloves down on the floor.

Then as she melted into his arms they sank down on the soft cushions of the sofa and forgot the elaborate tea with all its paraphernalia of silver tray, teapot, and boiling kettle that was waiting for them.

There were toast and brioches, hot scones and sandwiches, and several kinds of rich, sticky cake and quite a number of iced and cream ones.

Eloise was not hungry for food but for Rayburn's lips and the closeness of his arms, and the fire which was ignited in them burst into flame.

Rayburn was conscious only of the fragrance of lilies and Eloise's haunting Eastern perfume.

Now, adjusting his cravat in the mirror and aware that his high stiff collar had left a red mark on his neck, he suddenly felt stifled by the scent and the airlessness of the curtained Drawing-Room.

It was usual to have the curtains drawn at such a time, the excuse being that the lady required rest and to protect her eyes from the bright sunshine.

But Eloise's eyes, still gleaming with the fires he had aroused in her, were watching him.

"I love you!" she said. "Why cannot we be together this weekend? You can easily make an excuse to stay in London."

"I have made my arrangements now," Rayburn replied. "If we are together in London we shall be seen and there is enough talk about us already."

"Are you thinking of me or of yourself?"

"Of us both," Rayburn answered truthfully. "You have a husband and I have my political career."

"But George is in Paris," Eloise said, "and I know of a quiet little place where we could go, a hotel in the country where no one would see us."

Rayburn was suddenly still.

Eloise had never made such a suggestion to him before and he turned round to look at her in surprise.

"I want to be alone with you," she murmured passionately. "I want to stay in your arms all night. These snatched moments when we are afraid of every creak on the stairs are intolerable!"

Rayburn agreed with her there, but he was too wise to say so.

"There is no alternative," he said, "and you know

as well as I do what your husband would say if he found out."

Eloise Davenport knew this was true.

George might turn a blind eye to her love-affairs, and there had been many of them, and he undoubtedly enjoyed himself in a discreet manner, but if it was a question which affected his honour, if she was causing a scandal, that was something he would never tolerate.

Society was based on the Eleventh Commandment: "Thou shalt not be found out"!

It was taken for granted as part of the fun that there should be endless and inevitable *affaires de coeur,* but a scandal affected not only the two people concerned in it but the whole structure of the social scene.

The King, when Prince of Wales, had been in plenty of hot water in his life, as Rayburn knew, but never actually over his mistresses, and at the moment his love-affair with the wise and intelligent Mrs. Keppel actually had the approval of the Queen herself.

What Eloise was suggesting now was completely outside the rules of accepted behaviour and they both knew it.

"I think perhaps I am wise to go away as I intend to do this weekend," Rayburn said with a smile on his lips. "I can see that you are in a reckless mood when you are prepared to throw your bonnet over the windmill."

"I am throwing my heart at you."

She lay back against the cushions on the sofa and raised her hands above her head.

The soft green chiffon fell back to reveal the whiteness of her arms, and as she raised her face to his he could see the long line of her neck.

She looked very attractive and very seductive at that moment, and yet some critical part of Rayburn's mind flashed a warning that this spelt danger.

Eloise excited him and she stirred him more passionately than any other woman had done for a long time, but he knew that he was not in love with her.

He was well aware that she was self-centred, completely without scruples where her own desires were concerned, and had fundamentally a shallow character.

She concentrated every thought, every aspiration, every breath she drew on making herself more alluring and indulging her passionate emotions.

She had little self-control and as long as her beauty lasted there would always be men who would find her irresistible.

Something perceptive in Rayburn, of which Eloise had no idea but which was an intrinsic part of his personality, told him that this affair, like so many others, was coming to an end.

It had passed its climax and while the excitement and the exhilaration would continue for a little while longer, they would gradually begin to fade until his brougham would not be waiting outside Eloise's door at tea-time or at any other hour.

He looked at the clock.

"I must leave."

"Do not go yet. Please stay a little while longer," Eloise begged.

She held out her arms to him as she spoke, inviting him to kiss her, her dark eyes glinting, her red mouth provocatively inviting.

Rayburn avoided her clinging arms and taking her hand kissed it.

"Thank you for making me very happy, Eloise," he said in his deep voice.

"I shall see you tomorrow?"

"As I have told you, I am going to the country."

"But you could call before you leave. I must see you!"

There was something frantic in her tone because she knew he was being elusive.

Eloise found it impossible to believe that any man could refuse a request she made, especially Rayburn, to whom she was convinced she had given not only her body but also her heart.

"You could have luncheon with me," she said. "Just a quick meal here, or anywhere else you like."

"I will let you know," he said evasively.

She sprang from the sofa, and as he picked up his hat and stick her arms went round his neck.

"Oh, Rayburn," she said, her lips seeking his, "there has never been a more magnificent, more exciting lover than you! How can I ever bear to let you go, even for a few moments?"

He did not answer and she gave a deep sigh.

"If only you were my husband and I were your wife, how different everything could be! Rayburn, darling, you must love me forever, because I swear I cannot live without you!"

Because there was nothing else he could do, Rayburn kissed her, then resolutely he unlocked her arms from round his neck.

"I will send you a note first thing in the morning," he promised, "and now I really must go. The Prime Minister is waiting to see me."

That was not quite true although he actually had an appointment with several Cabinet Ministers in the House, but Eloise made no further effort to restrain him.

She knew that, however much she might mean in his life, politics came first.

"I love you!" she said as he reached the door. "Always remember that I love you. And think about me—think about me, Rayburn, all the time."

It was difficult for Rayburn not to do so as he drove away in his brougham, conscious that his clothes were fragrant with her scent and the touch of her lips still lingered on his.

He suddenly felt irritated because he had wasted the afternoon when he might have been riding in the sunshine or playing tennis.

The overscented atmosphere of Eloise's Drawing-Room made him feel as if he had eaten a surfeit of *foie gras* and in consequence felt slightly sick.

With an effort he forced himself to think of the meeting that lay ahead of him.

At the same time, he decided that nothing and no-one would prevent him from being the Earl of Croxdale's guest the following day.

* * *

Eloise Davenport received Rayburn's note on her breakfast-tray and her maid carried into her bed-room a huge basket of exotic orchids which he sent her at the same time.

She slit open the envelope with an eagerness which was belied by the expression in her eyes.

She knew only too well what she would read, and Rayburn's apologies for being unable to cancel his weekend in the country were as inevitable as the fact that he wrote no word of love.

Eloise had been aware since she first knew him that he was far too intelligent to commit himself on paper.

She was quite certain that there was no woman with whom he had ever been associated who was left with any incriminating mementos of their love-affair.

It was easy to be critical, but she admitted to herself that her whole body ached for him and she found him more attractive than any other man she had ever known in her life.

'Never have I been so wildly in love as I am now,' she thought, 'and never have I looked more beautiful!'

She glanced at herself in the gold-framed mirror of her dressing table, which was arranged so that she could see her reflection while she lay in bed.

She wondered what Rayburn would feel if he saw her now, with her long dark hair falling over her white shoulders and the diaphanous night-gown trimmed with real lace offering no concealment of the rest of her body.

She looked at the orchids and thought they were a fitting tribute to her loveliness.

Many men had described her as resembling an orchid, exotic, exciting, and unpredictable.

Eloise stretched herself sensuously against her lace-edged pillows.

Rayburn would come to her on Monday, she

thought. Even if George was back, he would go to his Club at tea-time.

They would be together again, and remembering what had happened yesterday afternoon her breath came a ltttle quicker between her parted lips.

* * *

Rayburn Lyle finished with the House of Commons Committee of which he was Chairman early on Friday morning and decided to have a quick luncheon before he drove to Croxdale Park.

The trip in his new sixty-horse-power Mercedes which had been delivcred the previous week would take approximately three hours.

He decided that if he started at two o'clock he would be there at five P.M., which would be exactly the time that he was expected and would give his valet plenty of time to unpack before he had to dress for dinner.

He drove to the St. James Club, preferring to have luncheon there rather than anywhere else because its Chef was outstanding, and Rayburn was as particular over his food as he was over everything else.

There were several Members whom he knew in the high-ceilinged Dining-Room and he joined two of them.

They sat talking about the political situation and the disturbing aspect of Germany's clear intention to build so many battle-ships.

The conversation was so engrossing that when Rayburn glanced at his watch he realised it was getting on towards half past one, and if he was to leave at two o'clock as he intended he must hurry home to change his clothes.

He had risen to his feet and begun to say good-bye to his friends when an old acquaintance came into the Dining-Room.

Major William Garthwaite was a King's Messenger and therefore was closely in touch with Rayburn when he carried despatches from the Foreign Office to the Ambassadors in the various Capitals of Europe.

"Hello, Garthwaite," Rayburn said, holding out his hand. "I did not know you were back from Paris."

"I was coming to see you this afternoon, as a matter of fact," William Garthwaite replied.

"I am sorry, but I shall not be at home," Rayburn answered. "Is it anything important?"

"Nothing that will not keep until Monday."

"Then let it keep!" Rayburn said with a smile.

He would have turned away, but William Garthwaite's next words arrested him.

"You have heard the news about George Davenport, I suppose?"

"What news?" Rayburn Lyle asked.

"He had a heart-attack in Paris yesterday, and before I left last night they told me he was dead!"

"Good God!"

The words came jerkily from Rayburn's lips.

"It will be a shock for everyone," William Garthwaite said, "especially his widow."

He turned to answer a question from one of the men with whom Rayburn had lunched, and as he did so Rayburn walked away.

He could hardly credit that what William Garthwaite had told him was the truth, but he remembered now Eloise saying on various occasions:

"George fancies he has a bad heart, but it is nothing but indigestion because he eats and drinks too much!"

But it had obviously not been indigestion, and now George was dead and Rayburn had an uncomfortable feeling that he would be expected to do something about it.

Driving back in his brougham to Queen Anne's Gate, he felt as if suddenly when he least expected it a pit had opened at his feet and if he was not careful he would step straight into it.

Remembering that time was passing, he hurried up the steps of his house and the door opened even as he reached it.

"Everything is ready for you upstairs, Sir," the Butler said.

Rayburn Lyle had his hand on the banister when the man added:

"A note came for you a short time ago, Sir. I did not take it in myself, but I understand from Henry, who opened the door, that it is urgent and requires an answer."

Rayburn looked at the envelope on the silver salver which the Butler held out to him and knew only too well who had sent it.

There was no mistaking the expensive pale green writing-paper which Eloise used and her flamboyant hand-writing.

"You say it was Henry who took it in at the door?" Rayburn asked.

Henry was the boot-boy and odd-job man about the house. He was in fact a trifle stupid, although he could do his routine jobs quite effectively at his own pace.

"Yes, Sir."

Rayburn considered for a moment.

"Listen, Batesman," he said finally. "If anybody asks you later, I had left for the country before I could receive this note, and it is therefore still awaiting my return. Is that clear?"

"Quite clear, Sir."

"Very good. Be quite positive about what happened," Rayburn ordered as he hurried up the stairs.

Every mile that took him further away from London made him feel that for the moment at any rate he was escaping from Eloise.

He was aware that her note would have told him of George's death and, knowing her as well as he did, that she would already be presuming that as soon as she was out of mourning he would marry her.

Yesterday was not the first time that she expressed the wish that he could be her husband and she his wife.

She spoke of it continually in moments of intimacy.

In his long experience of women Rayburn knew that, because he in his turn had never expressed such a wish, Eloise was determined to ensure in every possible way that their love-affair would be a permanent one.

It was only Englishwomen, he thought with an irritation, who wanted love to go on forever and felt that an affair which was little more than a light flirtation should be eternal.

Even to think of it convinced him, as he had been convinced ever since he had known her, that the last thing he wanted was Eloise as his wife.

She was not at all the type of woman he envisaged himself eventually marrying and settling down with in his house in the country, or gracing his table at political dinners in London.

He was rather vague about exactly what his ideal would be, but she would certainly not be as fiery, impetuous, and overpassionate as Eloise was.

Nor would she make insatiable demands upon his manhood without being in the least concerned with his character or his personality.

Rayburn was very conscious of the "I am I" of Greek thought, which was something he had studied even before he went up to Oxford.

When he had a free moment to himself he liked to read philosophy. There were a few people with whom he talked seriously on such a subject, but they did not include amongst them a woman.

Vaguely he thought that one day he would fall in love, and if fate was kind she would be the type of woman whom he would wish to put in his mother's place and whom he would not only love and desire but also respect.

He thought as he journeyed towards Croxdale Park that perhaps "respect" was the operative word.

He wanted to respect a woman, and for the Eloise Davenports of this world, even while they amused him and he could for a time be extremely infatuated with them, he certainly had no feelings of respect.

At the same time he was well aware that this was going to be a very difficult situation to handle.

There was "no fury like a woman scorned," and he knew that if he did not offer Eloise marriage, although they must wait a year for the ceremony to take place, her anger and resentment would know no bounds.

"What the devil can I do?" he asked himself.

When eventually he drove his motor-car up the drive at Croxdale Park he had found no solution.

The Mercedes had gone splendidly, as both his chauffeur sitting beside him and his valet sitting behind averred.

"I should think we must have broken the record, Sir," the chauffeur remarked.

"Two hours and fifty-five minutes exactly!" Rayburn said, looking at his watch. "We will ask His Lordship if he has beaten that. I believe he has a Hispano Suiza."

"I'll have a look at it, Sir, while I'm here," the chauffeur answered with a grin.

Rayburn took off his goggles and left them on the seat of the car. Then he walked into the magnificent marble Hall where liveried footmen were ready to divest him of his light dust-coat and tweed peaked cap.

Underneath these he was attired in a grey summer suit which almost matched the colour of his eyes.

He looked extremely handsome as he moved through the long Drawing-Room with french-windows opening onto the terrace outside.

There were a number of guests already gathered there round a tea-table over which the Earl's sister, Lady Emily Daltrey, was presiding.

She was older than her brother, her hair was unashamedly dead white, and she made no effort to hide her age as did many other ladies present.

"I am delighted to see you, Lyle," the Earl said, walking along the terrace to greet him. "Did you have a good journey from London?"

"Excellent!" Rayburn replied. "It took me exactly

two hours and fifty-five minutes. I am hoping that I have equalled, if not beaten, your record."

"I am more than pleased to be able to inform you that I came down this morning in two hours and fifty-two minutes," the Earl replied. "Can it be possible that I have actually defeated 'Lucky Lyle'?"

"You have!" Rayburn admitted.

"There always has to be a first time," the Earl laughed. "I think you know everyone here."

Rayburn held out his hand to several acquaintances. Then with surprise he saw first Lady Brandon, then Viola.

He shook hands with the former, but as Viola raised her eyes to his he knew without being told that she was in trouble.

It was impossible to be mistaken about the appeal he saw in those strangely purple eyes or not to be aware of the coldness of her fingers and the manner in which they trembled in his.

He felt that she was silently calling out to him for help, and he pressed her hand reassuringly before he turned to greet a number of other acquaintances.

"It is quite a large party," the Earl said, "and we shall be larger tomorrow. The King is coming over to dine and bringing of course the delectable Alice Keppel with him."

"His Majesty is staying in the neighbourhood?" Rayburn enquired, not because he was particularly interested but because he felt that some comment was expected of him.

"Yes, he is staying at Blenheim and of course the Duke and Duchess of Marlborough will be coming with him."

"It will be delightful to see them both again," Rayburn remarked.

"That is what the Duke said when I told him you would be here," the Earl replied.

There was no chance of speaking to Viola before the ladies went upstairs to rest before dinner.

But with thirty people staying in the house Rayburn told himself there was bound to be an opportunity of getting her to himself and finding out what was perturbing her.

He was not to know that when she reached her bed-room she said a prayer of thankfulness that he was in the party.

"Thank you, God, thank you!" she said. "If anyone can save me he can! There is no-one else I can turn to!"

She had felt almost frantic as they had driven down from London in the motor-car that the Earl had sent for them.

Before they had left London Lady Brandon had exploded a bomb-shell that had shattered Viola more completely than if a real one had exploded at her feet.

She had come into the Study where her step-daughter was looking for a book that she wished to take with her to read at Croxdale Park over the weekend.

"I want to talk to you, Viola," she had said in her hard voice.

"What is it, *Madre?*" Viola asked apprehensively.

She was well aware that she had got off lightly the night before, and now she was afraid that her Stepmother was about to revile her once again for not having gone to prison.

Lady Brandon had walked across the room to seat herself in one of the leather arm-chairs.

"Sit down, Viola," she said.

Viola obeyed, sitting on the edge of the sofa and wondering frantically what was coming.

"I think you enjoyed yourself last night," Lady Brandon said surprisingly, "and I noticed how attentive the Earl was to you at supper."

Viola had in fact found it embarrassing that he had talked only to her.

He had ignored his other two guests and seemed once again to be encroaching upon her so that she felt herself shrinking away from him not only physically but mentally.

"He is obviously very pleased with you," Lady Brandon said, "and I can think, Viola, of no more splendid and better match than for you to become his wife."

"His wife?" Viola ejaculated. "But . . . of course not! Even if he asked me, he is much too old."

"I think he intends to ask you," Lady Brandon replied. "He has certainly singled you out in a most obvious manner, and the mere fact that he has invited us to Croxdale Park and is sending his motor-car for us is tantamount to a proposal of marriage."

"I am sure you are wrong, *Madre*," Viola said in an agitated voice. "I cannot . . . think that the Earl has any such . . . intention."

"He has always liked very young women," Lady Brandon said reflectively, as if she had not heard Viola's remarks. "His last two wives were débutantes when he married them."

"Two wives?" Viola exclaimed. "He has been married twice?"

"His first wife died in child-birth and I believe it affected him deeply," Lady Brandon replied. "She was twelve years younger than he was. His second wife was killed a year ago when she was out hunting. She was only nineteen and had not given him a child."

She paused to say:

"He needs an heir, and I am quite certain he will propose to you this weekend."

"I do not believe it . . . but I could not . . . contemplate accepting him," Viola said frantically.

Lady Brandon gave her a hard look.

"You are not of age, Viola, and I am your Guardian. Doubtless the Earl will speak to me first, and if he does I shall accept on your behalf his offer, with the utmost pleasure."

"I could not marry . . . anyone who is as . . . old as that," Viola said.

She was thinking of how she felt disgusted by

the Earl when he was too near her and knew that she had disliked him from the first moment they had met.

"He is one of the most eligible men in England," Lady Brandon said with satisfaction. "He is also a close friend of the King and a notable race-horse owner. He has in fact everything to recommend him and you are an extremely lucky girl, although God knows why he should want anyone as stupid as you as his wife."

"Perhaps if you told him how stupid I am he would not be . . . interested in me," Viola said.

"Do not be more of a fool than you can help!" Lady Brandon said scathingly. "I shall extol your virtues, if you have any, to the skies and hope that he will not find out how half-witted you are until the ring is on your finger."

"I will not marry him . . . I will not!" Viola cried.

"If you go against my wishes in this matter you will be sorry," Lady Brandon said menacingly. "I assure you, Viola, in this instance I intend to have my own way. It will be a triumph for you, and it will be very helpful to me."

Viola looked surprised.

"I cannot expect you to understand unless I put it in plain English," Lady Brandon remarked scathingly, "so let me spell it out for you. While you are no asset to our Movement at the moment and have bungled everything I have ever asked you to do, you could be of considerable assistance to us as the Countess of Croxdale."

Viola's eyes widened.

Now apart from getting her out of the house and being rid of her, she could understand why her Stepmother wanted this marriage.

"You will be able to help us financially," Lady Brandon went on, "and actually we have no Countess amongst our ranks. Once you are married, you could carry a great deal of weight amongst the people who really matter."

"The question does not arise," Viola said in a

shaking voice. "I . . . cannot and . . . will not marry
Lord . . . Croxdale."

Her Stepmother's eyes narrowed.

"Look at me, Viola," she said. "You know what I
intend to do to you if you refuse the Earl."

She spoke slowly and deliberately, and despite
every resolution to be brave Viola felt fear rising
in her throat.

Once, when she had defied her Stepmother, Lady
Brandon had beaten her almost insensible and she
had never forgotten it.

Even now she could feel the agony that the weals
from the whip had caused and how long they had
taken to heal.

Her eyes must have expressed the fear which
made her mouth dry and her heart pound furiously,
because Lady Brandon laughed.

"You will accept him!" she said. "And I shall be
waiting to congratulate you."

All the way down in the motor-car Viola had felt
panic-stricken at the thought of what lay ahead.

If only the bomb had gone off in Rayburn Lyle's
house and she had died as she wished to do!

Even the sight of Croxdale Park, magnificent and
awe-inspiring in the afternoon sunshine, did nothing
to mitigate the horror she felt for its owner. When he
came to greet them, smiling and genial, she tried to
tell herself she was exaggerating her feelings for him.

But as the Earl took her hand she knew that he
aroused in her an even more violent revulsion than
before.

"I have asked you here early," he said, "because
I have something to say to both of you before the
other guests arrive."

"What is that?" Lady Brandon asked.

Viola held her breath.

Surely he was not going to say anything in front
of her Stepmother? Surely she would have more time
to consider what her answer should be?

"I have just heard that His Majesty the King

will honour me by coming to dinner tomorrow evening," the Earl replied. "I feel there is no need to say this, but I know you will understand my anxiety, Lady Brandon, when I ask you and Viola not to speak of the Women's Suffrage Movement in front of him."

He paused before he added:

"You know His Majesty's feelings in the matter and I would not wish him to be embarrassed in my house by one of my guests."

Lady Brandon did not answer for a moment and Viola hoped wildly that she would prefer to leave rather than have her conversation curbed in such circumstances.

Then the Earl said softly:

"Of course I am prepared to be—grateful for your restraint."

There was no mistaking the innuendo behind the words, and as Lady Brandon met his eyes she smiled.

"And we will be grateful for your generosity."

They understood each other and then the Earl turned to Viola. But before he could speak to her another guest was announced and she was spared for the moment from anything he might have to say to her.

Upstairs in her bed-room Viola felt as if Rayburn was like a life-line to a drowning man.

"He will help me," she told herself. "I am sure he will think of something I can do . . . some way I can be . . . saved."

She felt as if the Earl were a great Ogre menacing her in a manner that was so frightening, so overpowering, that she found it hard to think clearly.

It was useless to try to tell herself that the feeling she had for him was just her imagination.

She had always known that there were people in the world who were repelled by one another or had a mutual antipathy which perhaps had been there in another existence.

She and her father had discussed it once, and he admitted that in his Court life there had been people he disliked on sight for no reason except that he knew unmistakably that they could never have anything in common, however much their interests intermingled.

"Papa would have understood," Viola said to herself.

But her father was dead and the only person to whom she could turn in her extremity was Rayburn Lyle.

She followed her Stepmother down to dinner, conscious, although it was no consolation, that she was looking her best in a gown of white tulle over a foundation of silver.

As she crossed the Drawing-Room Rayburn thought that she was like a white violet coming into flower bravely while the frost was still on the ground.

There was so piteous and pleading an expression in her eyes that he felt impulsively protective towards her.

It was something he had never felt for any other woman. And certainly the women with whom he had associated had not needed his protection.

They had needed a great many other things, but they were always superbly sure of themselves, goddesses who swept across the social firmament like comets with a tail of admirers behind them.

As he saw Viola standing quietly and wearing no jewels amongst the other women, glittering, it seemed, from head to foot, he had an absurd impulse to walk across the room, put his arms round her, and tell her not to be frightened.

He could almost see the expressions of astonishment on every face as he did so, and he told himself that she was in fact an extremely tiresome child who was always getting into scrapes of some sort.

It was time she grew up and stood on her own feet.

But he knew with a twist of his lips, that she was quite incapable of doing any such thing.

He was sitting nowhere near Viola at dinner and was in fact on the other side of the table, with two extremely attractive married women on either side of him.

They vied in being provocatively flirtatious all through the meal.

He was well aware that they were trying to entice him away from Eloise Davenport and the fact that she was absent this weekend made them both hope that he might show them more favour in the future.

He played the game they expected with all the skill and expertise for which he was famous.

But even so, his eyes kept going to the other side of the table where between the elaborate gold candelabra and floral decorations in *Sèvres* bowls he could see Viola's exquisite little face.

She was talking seriously and politely to the gentlemen on either side of her.

There was no doubt that they both found her unexpectedly interesting and actually Rayburn's were not the only eyes that turned in her direction.

Viola was vividly conscious that at the end of the table the Earl was watching her as he had done the night he had taken her out in London.

She tried not to look at him, but she was acutely aware of his glance and felt as if his eyes bored into her and hypnotised her, leaving her with no hiding place from him.

The dinner seemed to be interminable, but at length Lady Emily gave the signal for the ladies to withdraw and Viola gave Rayburn a despairing glance as being the youngest she was the last to leave the room.

In the Drawing-Room there was a great deal of spiteful and amusing gossip in which Viola was not expected to join.

She heard a very lovely Peeress say to the lady next to her:

"I heard before I left London that our host was at the theatre the other night with a young girl in whom he was obviously interested."

Viola held her breath.

"I wonder who that could have been?" the other lady replied. "But then he has always liked them very young—cradle-snatching, I call it!"

The first speaker laughed rather spitefully as she replied:

"Obviously the noble Earl's idea is to 'catch them young and tell them nothing.'"

"They would have to be very young indeed not to recognise what he is like!"

Again there was that tinkling laughter that seemed somehow more damaging than unkind words, and a few minutes later the gentlemen came into the Drawing-Room.

Bridge-tables had been set up at one end of the room and the Earl started to arrange his guests round them.

Casually Rayburn approached Viola and said in a bored voice:

"Do you happen to play piquet?"

"Yes, I do," Viola answered.

"Then let me challenge you to a game."

They sat down at an empty table before the Earl realised what they were doing.

He came across to them as Rayburn began arranging the cards.

"I wanted you to play bridge, Lyle," he said with a sharp note in his voice.

"I would like to do that later," Rayburn replied, "but I have promised Miss Brandon that I will try to beat her at piquet, at which I believe she is an expert."

"And I will be delighted to give her a game," the Earl said.

"Of course," Rayburn replied, "but perhaps you could take my place at the bridge-table in the meantime."

The Earl was obviously not pleased at having his arrangements altered, but as Rayburn was already dealing the cards there was nothing he could do but return to his other guests.

Holding the cards in his hand and looking as if he was studying them, Rayburn said:

"What has upset you?"

"You knew there was . . . something?" Viola asked in a low voice.

"I am beginning to recognise the symptoms," he replied.

There was no sting in his words and he smiled as he spoke. For a moment her own expression altered and he thought there was a glint of hope in her eyes.

He told himself that he had never known a woman whose eyes were so revealing.

Though he might disbelieve the nonsense novelists talked about the eyes being the "mirrors of the soul," he was prepared to credit it where Viola was concerned.

The expressions swept across her face like the waters of a clear stream and now he saw that she was desperate as she pleaded with him, saying:

"Help me . . . please . . . help me! I do not . . . know what to do . . . and there is . . . no-one else I can tell."

"What has happened?" he asked. "Put down a card while you are speaking. It does not matter which one you choose, but we must appear to be playing."

She did as he told her. Then she said:

"My Stepmother thinks that . . . Lord Croxdale intends to . . . propose to me this weekend!"

For a moment Rayburn looked at her incredulously as if he thought she must be joking. Then he knew that she spoke the truth.

The Earl would never have invited Lady Brandon to this sort of house-party or Viola, who was the only young girl present, if his intentions were not serious.

Looking at Viola, Rayburn realised all too clearly that she was exactly the type that would attract the Earl.

He remembered too that there had been a lot of

jokes in the Club and at other places about the Earl's penchant for very young women.

Rayburn had paid no attention to them, he was not interested in gossip of that sort. But once he had visited a somewhat disreputable night-haunt with some of his friends after a bachelor-dinner for a man who was about to be married and he had seen the Earl.

He had been accompanied by a girl so young that she was little more than a child, and there had been some unpleasant remarks made by the other men in the party.

It all came back to him now and, looking at his host thickening with middle-age and with lines of debauchery under his eyes, Rayburn could understand what Viola was feeling.

"Are you sure?" he asked, because he knew she was waiting for him to speak.

"He has not . . . said anything," she answered, "and I tried to think that my Stepmother may be mistaken. But he keeps . . . looking at me and when he took us out to . . . supper the other night after the theatre . . . he kept touching me."

It was just what he might have expected, Rayburn thought savagely, and somehow it was sacrilege to think of the Earl with this ethereal, delicate white violet of a girl.

"Help me . . . please help me!" Viola pleaded. "I am . . . frightened . . . I am always saying that to you . . . but I felt somehow you would . . . understand."

"I do understand," Rayburn said. "Play a card! He is watching us."

Viola did so and after a moment without looking at her he said:

"I suppose your Stepmother would not let you refuse him?"

"She will half kill me if I do," Viola said, "and I could not stand up against her for long . . . you know I am . . . frightened of pain."

There was a quiver in her voice and an expression

in her eyes which made Rayburn's lips set in a hard line.

He loathed cruelty and he knew that what he was seeing was the torture of a small, defenceless animal which could not protect itself.

"I know I am a . . . nuisance," Viola said in a low voice, "and you do not want to be . . . bothered with me when you have . . . that lovely lady to think about . . . but . . ."

Her voice died away and Rayburn realised that she was speaking of Eloise Davenport—Eloise, who was waiting for him, stalking him in the same way that the Earl was stalking Viola.

They were in the same boat. They both found themselves in an impossible situation from which it would be difficult to escape.

Then suddenly, as clearly as if someone had spoken out loud, he knew the answer.

He looked at Viola and there was an expression in his eyes that made her heart leap.

"I have a solution!" he said with a note of triumph in his voice. "I know exactly what we must do! We must get engaged!"

CHAPTER FIVE

Rayburn saw Viola looking at him with an expression of surprise and incredulity.

"Trust me," he said quietly, and knew without her answering that she did.

He glanced across the room.

All the other twenty-eight guests were sitting round the bridge-tables, intent on their cards.

He threw those he held in his hand onto the table and said:

"Come, we will go out onto the terrace."

Obediently Viola followed him and they walked out through one of the french-windows onto the wide terrace where they had had tea.

There was a stone balustrade from which they could look over velvet green lawns and colourful flower-beds sloping down to a lake in the distance.

The sun had sunk, but it was still twilight with a crimson glow behind the tall oak trees in the Park. High overhead the first evening star was twinkling against the encroaching sable of the night.

As Rayburn walked to the balustrade to lean over it Viola joined him.

"We have little time to talk," he said in a low voice.

Viola lifted her face to his and he thought that while she was listening intently there was an expression of hope in her eyes which made him feel he must not fail her.

"If we announce our engagement," he went on, "it can be for an indeterminate period, until either the difficulties we are encountering at the moment fade away, or we can find some other solution to our problems."

"You are in difficulties too?" Viola asked.

He smiled at her.

"Very grave difficulties, but yours are the more immediate."

"I do not like to put you to so much . . . trouble."

"You are helping me, as I am helping you," he said firmly. "We will tell everyone we are engaged and it will then be impossible for the Earl to approach you."

"My Stepmother will be very angry," Viola said, "but I shall no longer be . . . afraid."

"Then what have you to lose?" Rayburn asked lightly.

He saw that she was still worried and he asked:

"What is it?"

"It is just that I do not . . . want to be a . . . nuisance to . . . you."

"As I have already said, you will not be a nuisance, but a very great help."

He spoke positively and he saw her expression change to one of gladness.

"You are so kind . . . so very kind . . . I knew as soon as I saw you that you were the one person who could . . . save me."

"You were sure of that?" he asked in surprise.

"Very . . . very sure," she answered.

They heard someone come from the french-windows behind them and Viola turned her head quickly, expecting to see the Earl. But it was Lady Brandon, and as she advanced across the terrace Viola could see the anger in her eyes and the tight line of her mouth.

Almost instinctively she moved a little nearer to Rayburn, but he was smiling as he spoke before Lady Brandon could do so.

"This is most opportune," he said, "that you should be the first person to wish us happiness."

His words surprised Lady Brandon so that it seemed as if she were jerked by astonishment into a statue-like stillness.

"What do you mean . . . ?" she began, only to be interrupted by Rayburn, who continued:

"Viola has made me the happiest man in the world, and of course we hope we may have your blessing."

There was just a suspicion of a mocking note in his voice, and it would have been difficult not to notice the fury which contorted Lady Brandon's face.

Then, as no-one spoke, Rayburn realised that she suddenly became aware that although she had lost the Earl as Viola's prospective husband she had in fact gained the Under-Secretary of State for Foreign Affairs.

It was an effort nevertheless for her to force a smile on her lips.

"It is certainly unexpected!" she said. "I had no idea you knew each other."

"I have known Viola for some time," Rayburn replied airily, "and of course I was a great admirer of her father."

This silenced any further protests and Lady Brandon turned to her stepdaughter to say:

"Then I must give you my good wishes, Viola, and hope that you will be very happy."

There was just a suggestion in her voice that she would be surprised if she was, but Viola was too relieved to be critical.

"Thank you," she said quietly.

"I came out to rebuke you both for making yourselves conspicuous," Lady Brandon said. "But I suppose now I must concede that there was some excuse for it."

"Every excuse," Rayburn remarked.

"I must go back to my bridge," Lady Brandon said. "I suppose you do not wish to keep this momentous news a secret?"

"Of course not!" Rayburn replied. "And with your permission I will put a notice in the Court Circular of *The Times*."

Lady Brandon did not reply.

She was hurrying back into the Drawing-Room and Rayburn turned to Viola with a smile.

"We are over the first hurdle."

"You were wonderful," Viola cried. "I thought she would be angry, but then I think she realised how ... important you are."

He was pleased that she was intelligent enough to interpret in the same way that he had the manner in which Lady Brandon had taken the news of their engagement.

They both knew there was still the Earl to contend with, and as if thinking of him conjured him up like an evil genius they could see him through the open window speaking to Lady Brandon in the centre of the Drawing-Room.

A few seconds later he came out to join them, and there was no mistaking that the news of their engagement had not only surprised but also infuriated him.

"What is this I hear?" he asked Rayburn with a hostile note in his voice. "You are engaged to Viola? Why was I not told about it?"

"For the simple reason that we were not sure of our feelings until this evening," Rayburn replied. "But in this perfect setting it is impossible not to feel romantic."

The Earl gave him a sharp glance as if he suspected that there was some other explanation, but had not the slightest idea what it could be.

Then he turned to Viola and took her hand in his.

"Are you sure, my dear," he said, "that you are not being somewhat precipitate in becoming engaged so young?"

"I am nearly nineteen."

"Still not very old to take such an irretrievable step," he said. "However, as Lyle says, it is a very romantic night."

He was putting a good face on it, but there was no mistaking the note of anger underlying his words or the expression in his eyes which made Viola avoid looking at him.

"Well, we must celebrate this world-shattering event," he said, "and of course make everyone aware of your glad tidings."

If he expected either Viola or Rayburn to shrink from an immediate public announcement, he was mistaken.

"They will all know sooner or later," Rayburn replied good-humouredly, "so why not now?"

It was as if he challenged the Earl and after a moment he replied: "Why not?" and led the way back into the Drawing-Room.

He advanced into the centre and looking towards the bridge-players said in a loud voice:

"Your attention, my friends! I have just learnt that my two attractive young guests, Viola and Rayburn, have decided to embark on the tempestuous sea of matrimony. I know you will wish to congratulate them."

There were cries of astonishment from the guests at every table except Lady Brandon's, where she must already have imparted the news to her fellow-players.

Bridge was abandoned for the moment, as everyone gathered round to shake Rayburn by the hand and kiss Viola.

The servants brought in champagne and their health was drunk with due ceremony before the excitement was over and everyone returned to their bridge.

Rayburn took Viola by the hand and drew her towards a sofa at the far end of the room where nothing they said could be overheard.

She sat down beside him and he noticed that although she was rather pale her eyes were shining.

"What happens now?" she asked.

"Nothing," he answered. "We go back to London on Monday, and are vague, extremely vague, about the date of our marriage. It is quite usual, in any case, for people to wait six months and by that time

we can think up a variety of excuses for not tripping
up the aisle."

Viola did not reply.

He was lying back on the sofa and she was sitting on the edge of it, her back very straight, her
fingers locked together in her lap.

She looked very young and at the same time
very lovely, and he thought with satisfaction that at
least he had saved her from the Earl.

But he knew without being told that she was
still worried.

"What is perturbing you now?" he enquired.

"I am afraid that my Stepmother will make me
do things which might damage your . . . career."

"You are thinking of me?"

"Of course . . . how can I think of . . . anything
else when you have been so kind?"

"You certainly have a point there," he said. "I
will speak to Lady Brandon, and I think it would be
clever if you make it quite clear that if she creates a
scandal I might be forced, for the sake of my future,
to break off our engagement."

"It may . . . damage you anyway, just to have . . .
my name connected with . . . yours."

"You have hardly done anything reprehensible as
yet," he smiled, "and frankly I am prepared to take
the risk."

"I would never . . . never . . . forgive myself if this
hurt you."

"You are very sweet," he answered caressingly,
"but I promise you I can take care of myself and
all I want is to see you looking happy and carefree."

She flashed him a smile which was like the sun
coming through the dark clouds.

"I am so lucky . . . so very, very lucky . . . to have
found you. I did not believe there was a man in the
whole world who would be as kind to me as you
have been."

"I think you will find that quite a number of
men will be only too willing to assist you," Rayburn
said a little drily.

His words made Viola glance at the Earl, who was sitting facing them at one of the tables.

"You are . . . different," she said. "I never feel afraid when I am with . . . you."

"I hope I can always live up to that reputation," Rayburn said. "You are making me feel like a Knight who has rescued a damsel in distress."

"That is exactly what you have done," Viola said. "I was . . . frantic . . . panic-stricken all the time we were driving here."

Her head dropped a little and she said in a low voice:

"I kept wishing that the . . . bomb had gone off in your house, and I had been . . . killed."

"You are not to talk like that," Rayburn said. "Do you hear me? You are never to say such things again. I have saved you, Viola, let me see—is it three times? And you know now that if necessary I can save you a further fourth or fifth!"

Viola raised her head to look into his eyes.

"You are so . . . .wonderful," she said, "so unbelievably . . . wonderful!"

There was a little throb in her voice that was very moving. Then as her eyes met Rayburn's it was difficult for either of them to look away.

He told himself that he was watching the expression in those dark, purple depths.

Yet there was something else, something which made him feel again that he would like to put his arms round her and protect her from everything that made her so frightened.

With an effort he said with a smile:

"Gratitude is not owed all on your side. As I have already said, I for my part equally need you."

Viola drew in her breath.

"Will the . . . lovely lady you were with at Roehampton House be very . . . angry when she . . . hears of our engagement?"

It was to be expected, Rayburn told herself, that Viola was too perceptive not to realise that the help she was giving him was somehow connected with Eloise Davenport.

He chose his words with care.

"I think Lady Davenport will be somewhat surprised," he said, "just as the guests here were surprised when they heard the news a few minutes ago. But I do not wish you to trouble your head about it."

"Do you mean that it is . . . wrong for me to speak about her?" Viola asked with the naïvety of a child.

"I hope we can always speak frankly on any subject," Rayburn replied. "At the same time, when in the past a man has been close friends with someone you describe as 'a lovely lady,' it is always wise for his future wife to know as little about her as possible."

"I understand," Viola said. "And you must tell me if I make mistakes or do anything which might embarrass you. I am very anxious to behave exactly as you would wish me to do."

Rayburn smiled at her tenderly.

He liked the way she said the right things. At the same time, she was original and different in every way from what he would have expected of so young a girl.

"It is because she is so sensitive and perceptive," he told himself.

He realised that one of the reasons why he had grown tired of so many of the women with whom he had been infatuated was that after a time there were no surprises.

They were in fact palpably obvious in everything they said and in everything they did.

The Earl rose from the bridge-table to walk towards them.

"It is your turn now, Lyle," he said, "and I hope you are luckier than I was in the last rubber."

"I have already lived up to my nick-name," Rayburn said provocatively.

He knew the words annoyed the Earl, but he could not help feeling that he had scored as he walked towards the bridge-table.

The Earl seated himself on the sofa beside Viola.
For the first time she was not afraid and could face
him with her chin held high and a smile on her lips.

"Are you feeling very happy?" the Earl asked.

"Very!" Viola replied.

"I had no idea you knew Rayburn Lyle. You did
not greet him very effusively when he arrived here
this afternoon."

Viola found the answer to this without any difficulty.

"I had not yet told my Stepmother what I felt
about him."

It was an explanation which the Earl could accept and after a moment he said:

"Shall I tell you how bitterly disappointed and
upset I am at learning you have decided to marry
someone else?"

"I do not ... think I ... understand."

"I thought you would have realised the other
night that I had fallen in love with you," the Earl said.
"It was love at first sight, Viola, and I will tell you now
that I intended this weekend to ask you to be my
wife."

"I am sorry if I have ... hurt you."

"It is worse than being hurt," the Earl said. "I
feel deprived, cheated out of something that I thought
of as already belonging to me."

There was a note of passion in his voice which
made Viola tremble. Then she remembered that there
was nothing he could do to her. Rayburn would protect her.

"I can only say again how sorry I am," she answered after a moment.

"Sorry enough to change your mind?" the Earl
asked. "I have so much to offer you, Viola, so much
more than Rayburn Lyle, rich though he is, can give
you."

He paused to add:

"There is an old adage that says: 'Better an old
man's darling than a young man's slave.' That is what

you would be if you married me, Viola—my darling
—and I know that I could make you love me."

With difficulty Viola prevented herself from shuddering obviously. Then with a courage which demanded an effort she said:

"I am very honoured that you should say such
things to me; at the same time, I am engaged to Rayburn and I think he would not approve."

"Damn him!" the Earl said violently. "He has
pipped me at the post and I dislike losing a race. I
want you, Viola, make no mistake about that, and I
shall do everything in my power to make you change
your mind before you actually become Lyle's wife!"

With an effort at dignity Viola rose to her feet.

"I think Your Lordship will understand that I am
rather tired after the long journey here," she said.
"Will you excuse me if I retire to bed?"

"Yes, of course, if that is what you wish," the
Earl replied, "but you will not be able to run away so
easily another time."

Viola walked towards the door.

As she reached it the Earl opened it for her and
she looked back to where Rayburn was sitting playing
bridge.

She waved her hand to him and he rose to his
feet, then she walked into the marble Hall with the
Earl beside her.

She was not afraid because she knew there would
be footmen on duty, and as was the regular custom in
country houses even when they had electric light
there was always a row of candles waiting for the
guests on a table at the bottom of the stairs.

It was a tradition which went back for generations. Viola took the candlestick which a footman
handed to her, then gave her other hand to the Earl.

"Good-night, My Lord, and thank you for inviting me to your beautiful house."

He took her hand in his but there was nothing
he could say with several servants listening.

"Good-night, Viola," he said.

He kissed her hand, and although she disliked the touch of his lips it did not frighten her as it would have done earlier in the evening.

She walked slowly up the stairs and did not look back even though she knew the Earl was watching her from the Hall below.

When she reached her bedroom she locked the door.

* * *

The Sunday papers carried the news of Lord Davenport's death in Paris, and Rayburn was well aware that some members of the house-party were looking at him speculatively.

They were wondering if he could have known of this tragedy before he arrived at Croxdale Park; and if so, they could not understand why he should have become engaged to Viola Brandon.

A number of women in the party insisted on talking to him about it, hoping, he knew, to watch his reaction and find some answer to the questions which puzzled them.

"Eloise will hardly be broken-hearted," they said. "At the same time, George was a complacent husband. He never objected to her beaux and was obligingly away from home quite a considerable amount of time."

"I think Lady Davenport was fonder of her husband than most people imagined," Rayburn Lyle said drily.

He knew this answer surprised them, and instantly they were wondering in fact whether Eloise had spurned him in a manner which had made him jump precipitately into marriage.

The attractive ladies who had tried so hard to flirt with him the first evening were convinced in their own minds that no woman who had Rayburn Lyle in tow would be so foolish as to give him up for any other man, least of all a husband.

"Does Lady Davenport know you are engaged?" the pretty blonde enquired curiously.

He had no intention of letting the house-party know, but he had written a letter to Eloise and sent it to London by a groom on Saturday afternoon.

He thanked her for the pleasure their friendship had brought him and added that he felt sure she would wish him happiness with Viola.

"I feel it is time I settled down and had a wife to help me politically," he wrote, "and Viola will give tremendous assistance in this and every other way!"

It was a letter into which Eloise could read as much or as little as she liked; but there was nothing in it to proclaim to an outsider that they had been lovers.

"Everyone will know about it on Monday," Rayburn replied in answer to the pretty blonde. "It will be in the Court Circulars of both *The Times* and *The Post*."

"Perhaps that will break Eloise's heart even more effectively than George's death," the blonde ventured.

"Are you not being rather feline?" Rayburn asked.

"As I expect you find most women are," she answered impudently. "The trouble with you, Mr. Lyle, is that you are far too attractive and too handsome to be let loose amongst the susceptible other sex."

"You flatter me quite outrageously," he said, "and although it is splendid for my ego it is certainly bad for my morals!"

"You will have to behave more circumspectly once you are married," the pretty blonde admonished, "for a little while at least!"

There was an invitation in the last words and Rayburn knew that marriage was not considered to be particularly restrictive where a man was concerned.

Women were different.

They were expected to conduct themselves with the utmost propriety for at least ten years, and then after they had produced several children they were allowed more licence so long as there was no open scandal.

For the first time Rayburn found himself thinking that the whole unwritten social code was somewhat barbaric.

How many broken hearts were there beneath the superficial veneer and how would Viola, so innocent and unsophisticated, cope with the world of pretence and subterfuge, of endless flirtations and accepted infidelity?

"She will grow used to it as she grows older," some cynical part of him told himself.

Then he knew he would hate to see her change and to watch her gradually become like all the other women in their incessant pursuit of men.

They totted up the number of hearts that were laid at their feet, in the same manner as their husbands totted up the number of pheasants they shot!

* * * *

Rayburn realised as the weekend proceeded in its leisurely, extravagant manner that Viola's purity made her stand out like a steady white light amongst the iridescent hues which shone from the other women.

There was something spiritual about her, he told himself, that he had never found in a woman or ever imagined to find in someone so young. She was also far more intelligent and better-read than he had suspected at first.

He realised that she had been so much in the company of her father, who was a clever man, that she was educated as few other girls of her age were.

Because they were engaged they were allowed a freedom which would never have been permitted otherwise and Rayburn took advantage of it.

While the others were playing croquet he strolled with Viola through the rose-gardens and he even took her boating on the lake, finding it easy to talk as their boat drifted under the shades of some weeping-willow trees.

Viola told him what the Earl had said to her the first night when he had sat beside her on the sofa.

"My Stepmother was right," she said. "He intended to . . . propose to me and if you had not been here I would have been . . . obliged to . . . accept him."

"Do not be afraid of his threats to continue pursuing you," Rayburn said. "There is nothing he can do."

"You are . . . sure of that?"

"Quite sure," he replied, "and he will not risk an open quarrel with me."

He smiled before he added:

"For which I am thankful! Otherwise I might, if we had lived fifty years ago, have been obliged to fight a duel with him on your behalf."

"I should have hated that," Viola said. "Suppose he had killed you?"

The thought of it was suddenly disturbing and she hardly listened as Rayburn replied gaily:

"You are not very complimentary! If this were a romantic novel, I should undoubtedly be the victor and kill him."

But Viola was thinking how desperately she would miss Rayburn, not only because he was protecting her, but also because when he went out of her life, perhaps it would be as suddenly as he had come into it.

It was an idea that persisted all during the day and kept ringing in her ears when she went to her bed-room to rest after tea and when she came down to dinner.

She was well aware that she had seen more of Rayburn over the weekend than she was ever likely to see of him again.

When they returned to London he would be busy at the House of Commons, and he had already told her that he had a great many official engagements the following week.

Perhaps he would occasionally call to see her in Curzon Street, although it would be quite impossible for her to go to his house unless she was chaperoned.

If he was at the House of Commons they would not be able to dine together and, although they would be asked together to a number of social functions, such occasions certainly would not be conducive to an intimate tête-à-tête.

After dinner she was relieved to see that everyone sat down at the bridge-tables and she hoped that perhaps there would be a chance to talk to Rayburn alone.

The night before there had been sixty people at dinner when the King had been there. His Majesty liked bridge and although he sat in a separate room with Mrs. Keppel as his partner everyone was expected to follow the Royal example.

Viola could play bridge even though she disliked it, but she had not been placed at Rayburn's table, which she was certain had been deliberately contrived by the Earl.

'If we play tonight,' she thought, 'I want to play with him, or perhaps we could play piquet and talk as we did the first evening.'

She looked at him eagerly as the gentlemen came into the Drawing-Room and he crossed to her side to ask, as she had hoped:

"What do you want to do?"

"I would like to talk to you." Then she added as an afterthought:

"But not if you would rather play bridge."

"I am delighted to do what you want," he replied.

He saw the light come into her eyes and thought it would be difficult for any man not to be flattered by the expression on her face.

Just for a moment it struck him that if she fell in love with him it might cause complications; then he told himself there would be time to worry about that problem later on.

"Shall we go and look at the pictures in the rooms adjoining this?" he asked.

"Could we do that?"

"It is something you have not done since you have been here," he answered, "and they are well worth seeing. The Earl's collection is notable."

"Then I would like to see them very much," Viola

answered, "and will you explain them to me? Papa taught me a little about art, but I feel I am not nearly as knowledgeable as I should be."

He put out his hand to help her to her feet and at that moment the Earl was beside them.

"My sister is very anxious that you should partner her, Lyle," he said. "As you know, she is the best player in my family and she tells me that you are outstanding."

"Lady Emily flatters me," Rayburn said, "but I should be grateful if you would make my excuses, as I have promised to show Viola your pictures."

"That is something that as your host you must allow me to do," the Earl said. "It is very remiss of me, Viola, that I have not taken you round before."

"Perhaps we could all go together," Rayburn suggested. "I fancy myself as a connoisseur of art and, as I have already told Viola, your collection is famous."

The Earl raised his eye-brows.

"It would surely be somewhat unkind to leave one table with only three players and my sister without a partner."

Rayburn realised he had been driven into a corner from which at the moment he could not extract himself.

Without making a scene there was little he could do, and he hoped that Viola would have the sense to say that now after all she felt too tired to see the pictures.

But as he moved away Viola found herself unable to refuse the Earl's insistence, and taking her arm he drew her into the Ante-Room to the Drawing-Room where the King had played bridge the night before.

"All the pictures I have hung here," he said, "are Dutch. I pride myself on having some fine works by Cuyp and by Van der Heyden and am almost sure that the one that I bought only last week is the most attractive I have ever seen."

He closed the door into the Drawing-Room as

he spoke and Viola moved quickly from his side to look at the pictures which were all well hung and well lit.

"I like the Dutch artists," she said.

"And I like you," the Earl replied. "You are far more beautiful than any picture in my collection and I am still wanting, more than I have ever wanted anything, to acquire you."

"I hoped you would not . . . speak like this . . . again."

"You cannot prevent me from expressing what I feel," the Earl said, "and where you are concerned, Viola, I feel very strongly that I have been defrauded of a great treasure, of something of such value that it is impossible to put a price upon it."

He came a little closer to her as he spoke and Viola hastily moved away.

She turned to look at another picture but found it difficult to focus her eyes on it as her heart had begun to beat frantically with fear.

"I want to show you some pictures which will be much more to your taste," the Earl said.

Because she felt somehow relieved that she could move and he was not standing so close to her, Viola followed him across the Ante-Room.

They entered another Drawing-Room, which was decorated in blue and silver and where all the pictures were French.

There was a very beautiful Boucher and some attractive Fragonards. Viola wished that Rayburn was with her and that they could look at them together.

Then as the Earl shut the door she realised too late that she should not have come so far from the Drawing-Room.

In the Ante-Room there was only one door between her and Rayburn and if she screamed he would have heard her; but here the room, which was obviously little used, seemed very quiet and isolated.

Because she felt nervous she began to move away from the Earl, which meant she went further into the room.

"You are lovelier than any picture," the Earl said.

There was a thickness in his tone which made Viola feel a new flicker of fear mounting within her breasts.

"I . . . think we should . . . go back now," she said incoherently. "Rayburn will not . . . want . . ."

"I am not concerned with what Rayburn wants —I am concerned with you! Listen to me, Viola. . . ."

She was still, but she would not turn her head.

"Look at me," the Earl said. "I want you to look at me."

Because it seemed childish not to do so, Viola turned her head towards him and fearfully her eyes met his.

There was an expression on his face that made her draw in her breath.

"You are mine!" the Earl said. "You were always meant to be mine and Rayburn is not really interested in you. He is merely using you to escape from Eloise Davenport, who will expect him to marry her now that her husband is dead!"

He spoke sharply, almost brutally. Then as Viola's eyes widened he went on:

"That was why Lyle asked you to marry him— you might as well know the truth—so that he could avoid his obligations to a woman with whom he has been living in what I presume you would call 'sin' for the last six months. He is not interested in you, Viola, nor does he love you as I do."

He drew near her as he said:

"Marry me and I will make you very happy. I will teach you more about love than young Lyle could ever do."

The last words were smothered as violently he pulled her into his arms and tried to kiss her lips.

He succeeded only in touching her cheek, and for a moment she felt as if she had been mesmerised into immobility by what he had been telling her, but then she began to fight.

She struggled convulsively to avoid his mouth

and pushed with her hands against his chest to prevent him from holding her closer and even closer.

As she did so she realised how weak and helpless she was against his superior strength.

She knew too that at the touch of her the Earl had lost control of himself and was exerting all his strength to compel her to his will.

It was only a question of seconds, Viola thought, before he would kiss her on the lips, and she felt so revolted with the horror of it that she gave a scream of terror.

Even as her voice rang out not very effectively in the big silent room she knew that she was powerless and that the Earl had in fact turned into a beast of prey.

He was kissing her cheeks hungrily and demandingly and although she tried to turn her head further and further away from him his lips were nearly touching hers.

It was then that she heard the door open and a voice ask angrily:

"What the hell is going on here?"

It was Rayburn and she knew as her heart leapt at the sound of his voice that once again he had saved her.

She felt the Earl's arms relax. Then with a last effort of her dying strength she fought herself free.

She ran towards Rayburn, holding on to him frantically, feeling it impossible to speak, difficult to breathe.

Her hands fastened desperately onto the lapels of his evening-coat and she hid her face against his shoulder as his arms went round her.

Rayburn did not speak, he merely looked at the Earl, who was brushing an imaginary speck of dust from his coat.

The silence was explosive until at last the Earl said:

"There is no point in making a scene about this, Lyle."

"I agree," Rayburn replied, "and it would undoubtedly cause a great deal of comment if Viola and I returned to London tonight."

The Earl did not answer and after a moment Rayburn said:

"We will leave very early in the morning and I hope neither of us sees you before we go."

The Earl's lips tightened at the insult but there was nothing he could do about it. Instead he turned and walked from the room, slamming the door behind him.

Viola was still holding convulsively on to Rayburn, her face hidden.

He could feel that she was trembling and her body was very soft beneath the chiffon of her evening-gown.

"It is all over," he said gently. "I hoped you would have the sense not to come into these rooms alone with him."

"I . . . I could not think . . . what to do. . . ."

Viola's voice was so low and hesitating that he could hardly hear what she said.

"Forget about it," he said. "You need never see him again."

He felt her relax her grip on the lapels of his coat, but she still hid her face and after a moment she said:

"He said horrible . . . things about you."

"What did he say?" Rayburn asked, anticipating the answer before Viola stammered:

"He said you were using me . . . to evade your . . . responsibility towards . . . Lady Davenport."

Rayburn's arms tightened for a moment.

"And if I am, it has nothing to do with Lord Croxdale," he said. "Come and sit down, Viola, I want to talk to you."

He drew her to the nearest sofa, and as she sat down he saw how very pale she was and the tragic look in her eyes.

"Are you . . . quite sure you are not doing this

just to . . . save me?" she asked. "Lady . . . Davenport
is so . . . beautiful . . . and I am . . . sure that she . . .
loves you."

Her eyes were fixed on Rayburn's face and he
knew that she was thinking of him and not of herself.

He decided that only the truth could meet the
situation.

"If Lady Davenport does love me," he said, "which
I very much doubt, I do not love her, Viola, and I do
not wish to marry her in any circumstances. I told you
that you were helping me just as I was helping you,
and I asked you to trust me."

"I do trust you . . . I trust you completely and . . .
absolutely," Viola said. "But I do not . . . want you to
hurt yourself simply because you were being so . . .
kind to me."

I am not as quixotic as you imagine," Rayburn replied, "and even if this were not a rescue operation as
far as you are concerned, I should be very glad, very
glad indeed, for you to rescue me as you are doing at
this moment."

"Do you . . . really mean that?"

"I mean it!" he answered.

She gave a deep sigh of relief. Then she said once
again in a frightened little voice:

"You will not . . . let him . . . come near me . . .
again?"

"I am going to suggest that you go to bed immediately," Rayburn said, "and lock your door. I intended
anyhow to leave for London immediately after breakfast tomorrow. I will take you with me in my motor-
car. Then there can be no dramatic interludes, such
as I have just witnessed, once I have left the house."

"You p-promise you will do that . . . even if my
. . . Stepmother says I am to . . . go with her?"

"I feel your Stepmother would consider my
chauffeur and my valet sufficient chaperonage in an
open car," Rayburn said drily. "And anyway engaged
couples have certain privileges."

"Then . . . thank you very much!"

Viola put up her hand to her cheek where the Earl had kissed her, as if she would erase even the memory of his lips.

Because he knew what she was thinking, Rayburn said:

"Forget it!"

"It was . . . horrible and more frightening than anything I can . . . imagine," she said. "It would have been worse . . . much worse . . . if you had not been here to stop it."

"Once again I have saved you!" he said with a smile.

He stood up and drew her to her feet.

"There will be nothing to frighten you after to-night—that I promise you!" he said.

"I am so . . . grateful . . . so very grateful," Viola murmured.

Her face was turned up to his, her eyes were very dark.

He looked down at her and thought it would be difficult for any woman to equal her strange, unusual beauty.

"Shall I tell you something, Viola?"

She waited, her eyes still on his face.

"I think we might enjoy being engaged to each other. There are lots of things we could do, and the fact that we do them together need not be only a pretence to deceive either your Stepmother or the Earl."

He saw the light he was waiting for come into her eyes.

"Do you mean that?" she asked. "I thought that when you went back to London you would not . . . wish to . . . see me and would not have any . . . time for me."

"I do want to see you and we must make time. Is that a bargain?"

"It would be . . . wonderful for me," Viola said simply.

"I will look after you and I will protect you."

Viola glanced over her shoulder towards the door as if she felt the Earl might be waiting for her on the other side of it.

Rayburn did not pretend to misunderstand her action.

"I doubt if he will approach you again," he said. "He knows I could make things very uncomfortable for him if I told the world he was deliberately trying to break up our engagement and steal my fiancée from me.'

His lips tightened. Then he said:

"Damnit! If I had any sense I would knock him down! But he is an older man, and I dislike scenes of that sort."

"P-please . . . do not do anything like that," Viola pleaded. "He is very important and he might . . . harm you."

"I doubt that," Rayburn replied. "At the same time we have behaved in a civilised way, even though as far as I am concerned it goes against the grain."

Viola sighed.

"I am sorry that once again I should . . . involve you in such a . . . difficult situation."

"You really seem to have a genius for it," Rayburn teased.

Then as he saw the consternation in her expression he added gently:

"Do not worry, I shall doubtless learn to enjoy such dramas! My life has been curiously uneventful until now."

He put his hand up to his forehead.

"First the bomb—then the Police Station—now rescuing you from the arms of a villain—I wonder what the next act will produce."

"I can only pray that I shall not be involved in any more," Viola said. "Oh . . . please believe me . . . I am ashamed and humiliated that all these things should have happened . . . and yet every night when I say my prayers I thank God that you are there."

There was something in the sincerity of her tone

which took the smile from his lips and made him look at her with a strange expression on his face.

"I thought you would say your prayers."

"Of course!"

"Yes, of course!" he echoed. "Well, I think you have been through enough for one night. Go to bed, Viola, and dream of all the nice things we are going to do when we get back to London. Forget Votes for Women and lascivious Earls, and think only of the things that violets think of, when they are sheltering under their leaves."

"That is what I am doing," she said, "sheltering under a leaf which is you . . . a very large protective leaf which is always . . . there when it is . . . wanted."

"I hope I always shall be," Rayburn smiled.

He walked across the room to open the door which led to the passage into the Hall.

He knew she would not go back to the bridge-players and he was quite certain that the Earl would make some plausible excuse for their absence.

He himself intended to make a brief appearance in the Drawing-Room, then also retire to bed.

He still had a lot of work with him which he had not completed during the weekend, and he would much rather work in his bed-room than converse with the Earl and his guests.

A footman was waiting with a lighted candle for Viola and as she took it she gave Rayburn her hand and he felt her fingers close involuntarily on his, as if she hated to let him go.

"Good-night, Viola," he said, "and sleep well. We will leave at nine o'clock."

"Nine o'clock," she repeated.

It seemed as she looked into his eyes that she was saying something very different.

He pressed her hand.

Then as she walked up the stairs, leaving him behind in the Hall, she knew positively and irrefutably that she loved him with all her heart.

CHAPTER SIX

The brougham stopped outside the house in Curzon Street and Viola stepped onto the pavement.

"Do not move, Carstairs," she said to the chauffeur, "it might stop the engine."

"Thank you, Miss," the chauffeur replied, and touched his crested cap as Viola ran up the steps.

She was smiling as she waited for the Butler to open the door and she felt that the sunshine was more golden than it had ever been before.

Every time she was with Rayburn she knew that she felt more and more in love with him.

Today, watching him at the luncheon-party he had given at his house, she had thought that it was impossible for any man to be more handsome or more attractive.

She was aware that he did not love her, but for the moment it was enough that she could love him.

She thought when they returned to London that she might never see him again, but this was the third time in a week that they had been together.

First he had escorted her to meet some of his aunts, and although it had been somewhat of an ordeal she had not really been nervous, because he was with her.

Another evening they had both been invited to a dinner-party with one of his Parliamentary colleagues. She had enjoyed the more serious conversation and it had been a thrill all of its own when Rayburn took her home after the dinner was over.

Today he had had to hurry back to the House as there was to be a debate on Foreign Affairs starting in the afternoon but as they left each other he had said:

"Are you going away for the weekend?"

She had shaken her head.

"Then perhaps we could do something together."

She felt her heart turn over with excitement because he wanted to see her, and it was with difficulty that she prevented herself from begging him to be more explicit or clinging to his hand when he said good-bye.

"I love him! I love him!" Viola told herself.

She crossed the Hall to enter her father's Study and to stand thinking of Rayburn with her hands to her cheeks.

She forced herself not to plan ahead; not to wonder what would happen when their pretended engagement came to an end.

All that mattered for the moment was that she could see him sometimes, hear his deep voice talking to her, and know that he was protecting and taking care of her.

Everything seemed to have changed since the moment that he had announced their engagement.

Now her Stepmother no longer ordered her to go to meetings or to take part in the Suffragette activities. Although Viola had an anxious feeling that she was biding her time until she was actually married, the relief of feeling free for the time being was inexpressible.

"I love him!" Viola told herself again.

She walked to the window to stare with unseeing eyes out into the sunshine which gilded the leaves of the shrubs in the rather dull little court-yard at the back of the house.

'If only we could be in the country together,' she thought. 'If only I could talk to him alone.'

Then she gave a deep sigh.

She was asking the impossible. She knew that.

Rayburn had saved her and himself from an intolerable situation, but in effect she meant nothing to him and he was not interested in her as a woman.

She thought of all the attractive ladies he had known, sophisticated, scintillating Society beauties and great hostesses.

She had learnt quite a lot about him in the past week: one thing everyone was ready to tell her by varying means was not only that Rayburn was a social success but that women fawned on him.

No-one put it bluntly or tactlessly, of course, but Viola could see the surprise in their eyes that he had chosen to marry someone so unsophisticated.

She caught snatches of conversation in which they referred by name to many of the great beauties who had all been close friends of Rayburn's in the past.

"Of course Rayburn has always been very gay...."

"I cannot think how you met Rayburn, he has always moved with the smart Marlborough House Set."

"Rayburn was there with—"

Viola used to hold her breath and out would come the name of some famous beauty whose pictures filled the illustrated papers!

And never, she told herself, never could she forget the allurement and the fascination of Lady Davenport when she had seen them together at Roehampton House.

How could she compete? How could she?

She realised she had been standing for a long time doing nothing and told herself severely there were still a lot of letters for her to answer.

Letters from school-friends who had seen the announcement of her engagement in the newspapers, letters from distant cousins and old friends of her mother's.

She took off her hat and screwing the long frills into the crown she put it on a chair and turned towards her father's desk, which was now stacked with her own correspondence. As she did so the door opened.

The Butler came in with a note on a silver salver.

"There's a carriage at the door, Miss, and the coachman's been told to wait for an answer."

Viola picked up the note and opened it.

She saw that the envelope was heavily outlined in black and the writing was in a hand she did not recognise.

Then she looked at the signature, giving a little gasp before she read the note itself.

June 25, 1907   24 Belgrave Square,
                                               London

Dear Miss Brandon

Your fiancé, Rayburn Lyle, and I are very old friends. I am therefore greatly looking forward to making your acquaintance and would appreciate it if you could find time to have tea with me this afternoon.

There are many matters I should like to discuss with you, including a suitable wedding-present for you both. I do hope that you can accept my invitation, as I may be leaving London shortly.

                                               Yours sincerely,
                                               Eloise Davenport

Viola stared at the flamboyant signature which covered nearly half the page and asked herself frantically what she should do.

She had no wish to meet Lady Davenport.

She felt they had nothing to say to each other, and she knew in her heart that she was afraid of meeting the beautiful, seductive woman who had looked at Rayburn from under her eye-lashes in such an alluring and at the same time possessive manner.

Then she told herself that once again she was being a coward.

Nothing could be more friendly or indeed more pleasant than the letter, and if she refused to go would not Rayburn think that she was being deliberately rude to one of his old friends?

She wanted to ask his advice. She wished it was possible for him to tell her what to reply, but he was by now in the House of Commons, where she could not reach him.

"Dare I refuse?" Viola asked herself. "It is what I want to do!"

She realised that the Butler was waiting. Then feeling somehow weak and helpless she took the course of least resistance.

"Please say I will be ready in ten minutes."

"Very good, Miss."

The Butler went from the Study and Viola sped upstairs.

All the time she was changing with the help of her maid into one of her more elaborate afternoon-gowns she wondered if she was doing the right thing.

"If I refuse," she argued with herself, "it would look as if I was jealous or spiteful, and I would hate Rayburn to think I was like that."

She hurried downstairs in under ten minutes' time, looking extremely attractive in a white gown trimmed with mauve ribbons and with bunches of mauve wistaria ornamenting her wide-brimmed hat.

But her eyes were worried and anxious and when the carriage reached Belgrave Square her fingers were trembling.

Lady Davenport's house was very large and impressive. It seemed to be scented with an exotic Eastern perfume which Viola vaguely thought reminded her of incense.

There were two footmen in attendance in addition to the Butler who led her slowly and pompously up the wide staircase to the double Drawing-Room on the first floor.

"Miss Brandon, M'Lady!" he announced.

Viola walked hesitatingly forward as a slim figure in black rose from an arm-chair which seemed to be banked by a profusion of Madonna lilies.

Dead-black mourning made most women look subdued, but where Lady Davenport was concerned it accentuated the fiery red of her hair, the dazzling white of her skin, and the green of her eyes.

As she advanced towards her hostess Viola thought that she looked more than ever like a bird of Paradise and she wondered how Rayburn could ever wish to escape from anyone so alluring.

"How sweet of you to come, Miss Brandon!" Lady

Davenport said, holding out a thin white hand which seemed almost too slender to carry the huge rings she wore.

"It was very kind of you to ask me," Viola said nervously.

"Do sit down," Lady Davenport begged, indicating a sofa near her chair.

Viola seated herself gingerly on the edge of it, feeling rather like a school-girl in the presence of an awe-inspiring head-mistress—or perhaps, she told herself, like a small, ineffectual rabbit being entertained by a snake.

Always perceptive where other people were concerned, she knew that while Lady Davenport smiled at her, her eyes were venomous and there was no real welcome in the touch of her hand.

"I felt that we have so much in common that it is essential for us to get to know each other," Lady Davenport said as the Butler and footmen carried in a tray laden with all the paraphernalia appertaining to the ritual of tea-making.

Graceful with every movement she made, Lady Davenport busied herself spooning the tea from the silver cannister into the teapot, pouring in the boiling water from the kettle, then placing a silver strainer over the delicate porcelain cups before the golden liquid flowed into them.

There were untold things to eat, sandwiches, scones, asparagus deliciously rolled in brown bread, and fish-paste in white.

There were fairy-cakes, madeira, cherries, plums and little mouthfuls of cream and icing which at any other time Viola might have found extremely delectable.

But she felt as if it was impossible for her to force a mouthful of food down her throat.

"Rayburn and I are such very old friends," Lady Davenport said when she had finished with the teacups. "I expect he has told you how much—how very much—we meant to each other."

"Y-yes ... of course," Viola answered.

"I do so hope he will be happy," Lady Davenport went on. "I expect you realise he is a very complex and in some ways difficult man."

She gave a light laugh.

"But what man is not? They are all difficult and of course all adorable. What would we do without them?"

She did not seem to expect an answer to this and Viola remained silent.

"I will be honest with you," Lady Davenport continued, "and say that I did not expect Rayburn to choose for his wife someone so young and—shall we say?—so inexperienced. Any man is difficult to keep amused and perhaps Rayburn is more difficult than others."

There was a sharp note in her voice as she spoke. Then as if she forced herself to continue in a lighter tone she said:

"However, love conquers all things, does it not? You must tell me, because I am so curious, when you first fell in love with each other."

Viola drew in her breath.

Now, she thought, the cross-examination was to begin."

"I . . . I think as . . . soon as we . . . met."

"And when was that?"

There was a little pause before Viola replied:

"Some . . . some time ago."

"It is so strange that Rayburn did not tell me," Lady Daveport mused. "He told me most things because we saw each other so often, but he never mentioned you, although I have an idea that he had met your Stepmother."

There was silence until Lady Davenport continued:

"And do you intend to go on with your Suffragette activities? You must feel very strongly on the subject of Votes for Women, having been brought up in such a household."

"It is my Stepmother's interest . . . not mine."

Lady Davenport raised her eye-brows.

"Somebody told me—I cannot remember who—that you have been at various of their meetings."

"Yes . . . of course," Viola answered, "but I do not think that Rayburn . . . approves."

"I am quite sure he does not!" Lady Davenport said firmly. "And if you were to be involved in such activities it would certainly harm him politically."

"Y-yes . . . I realise . . . that."

"Poor Rayburn!" Lady Davenport exclaimed. "I can imagine nothing more embarrassing than the Under-Secretary of State for Foreign Affairs having a wife in Holloway! You will have to be very, very careful not to embarrass him in such a manner."

"Yes . . . of course," Viola agreed.

"But I have always been told that your Stepmother is a very determined woman. . . ."

There was a pause and after a moment Viola said:

"I . . . think she understands now that I . . . cannot go on . . . helping her."

"I hope so!" Lady Davenport said. "Unless of course you were to win over Rayburn. How amusing if he were to champion the Women's Cause, and how alluring and attractive he would look at the head of one of your processions!"

Viola put down her cup and saucer and it rattled slightly as she did so.

"I think, Lady Davenport, I should be getting home," she said. "I have a lot of things to do. It was very kind of you to invite me."

"I am so glad you have enjoyed yourself," Lady Davenport replied. "We have had no time to discuss what I should give you as a wedding-present, but I assure you that I am giving it very serious thought. It must be something very intimate which dear Rayburn will appreciate from me."

There was something in the way she spoke which made Viola quiver.

She rose to her feet, knowing that she wanted nothing except to get away and be free of this woman whom she felt exuded venom with every word she spoke.

Yet there was nothing in her actual words to which she could possibly take exception.

Slowly and deliberately Lady Davenport rose to her feet.

"Good-bye, dear Miss Brandon," she said. "Let me say again what a pleasure it has been to meet you. The carriage will take you back."

As she spoke she rang a small silver bell which stood on the tea-tray and the door opened instantly.

"Thank you very much," Viola answered. "Good-bye."

As she walked across the Drawing-Room towards the door she felt as if her hostess's green eyes were boring into her back.

It was with difficulty that she managed to walk slowly down the stairs and step in an unhurried manner into the carriage waiting outside.

Only as she drove away did she draw a deep breath and feel as if she had been mauled by a panther.

"She is horrible! Beastly! Venomous!" she told herself. "But so beautiful! How could Rayburn not love her?"

She felt despairingly that it would be impossible for her ever to attract him after he had known Lady Davenport.

He might not wish to marry her, but how could be resist those curving red lips, those slanting eyes, and that white skin which looked like the petals of a magnolia?

'She is so assured, so poised, so sophisticated!' Viola thought unhappily. 'How gauche and awkward I must seem beside her!'

When she reached Curzon Street she felt as if the sun had gone and she was no longer happy as she had been when she came back from luncheon.

It was as if she was looking ahead into a future that was dark, grey, and empty, when Rayburn would leave her and she would have no-one to protect her.

Once again she went into her father's Study and sat down at the desk.

Somehow, although she tried, she could not make sense of the letters of congratulation.

All she could see was Lady Davenport's fascinating face and feel in some obscure manner to which she could not put a name that she was trying to hurt Rayburn.

"She will never forgive him," Viola told herself, "and somehow she will try to get even."

Then she told herself she was being imaginative. What could Lady Davenport do to Rayburn now?

He was free of her! His engagement had been announced and in a little while no-one would remark on his friendship with the delectable, green-eyed Eloise Davenport.

'Even so, she will do everything she can to get him back,' Viola thought prophetically, and now there was a sharp pain in her heart at the thought.

A vision came to her of Rayburn holding that slender, elegant body in his arms and kissing those red, curving lips.

"I will not think about it . . . I will not!" Viola told herself.

Jumping to her feet, she walked about the room as if just by being active she could keep away the thoughts which mocked and jeered at her.

'What have you to offer him? You who are so stupid, weak, and cowardly? A girl who knows nothing of the world?'

She could almost hear the words being said aloud and there was no escape from them.

It was after six o'clock when Viola realised she was still sitting in the Study and had done nothing since her return from Belgrave Square.

Her Stepmother had gone to a meeting at Wimbledon and should be back in half an hour or so.

Viola knew they were to dine alone tonight. Lady Brandon had already announced that she intended to

retire early as she had to leave the following morning
to be present at a rally at Oxford.

Vaguely Viola wondered if her Stepmother would
want tea when she returned, then thought it would be
too late. They would have dinner at eight o'clock
and Lady Brandon would undoubtedly wait until then.

She heard a footstep outside the door and thinking
that she must have returned she rose to her feet to
greet her.

The door opened, but it was the Butler.

"There are two Policemen in the Hall, Miss Viola,
who wish to speak with you."

"Two Policeman?" Viola echoed in surprise. "What
do they want?"

"They didn't say, Miss."

It must be something to do with her Stepmother,
Viola thought, and hoped that Lady Brandon had
not been involved in anything which would result in
publicity.

'Rayburn would not like that,' she thought.

She walked into the Hall to find the two Policemen
awkwardly holding their helmets.

"You wish to see me?" she asked.

"You are Miss Viola Brandon?"

"Yes."

"We've to arrest you, Miss, for causing a fire in a
house in Belgrave Square."

"Causing a fire?" Viola exclaimed in astonishment.

"Yes, Miss. It's been reported that after you called
to see Lady Davenport you started a fire in a downstairs room before you left the house and left a number of leaflets to show why it had been done."

"It is not true!" Viola gasped.

"I'm afraid, Miss, we must ask you to come with us
to the Station."

"There must be some mistake. I had tea with
Lady Davenport but when I left her I came home immediately in her carriage."

"You'll be able to make a statement when you
reach the Station, Miss."

"Will I have to . . . stay . . . there?"

Viola felt as if her voice came from a long distance away.

"That's up to the Officer in Charge, but I expects so, Miss."

Viola felt her heart pounding, the walls were swimming round her. Then with an effort she forced herself to think clearly.

"Would it be possible, before we go . . . for me to write a letter to my . . . fiancé?" she asked. "He is the Honourable Rayburn Lyle, Under-Secretary of State for Foreign Affairs."

The name obviously impressed the two Policemen, who looked at each other.

"I think that'll be all right, Miss," one of them answered, "as long as you don't try to leave the house."

"I will not do that," Viola answered. "If you wish you can come with me while I write the note."

As if they felt uncomfortable at the suggestion, they informed her that it would be all right and she ran to the Study.

She told Rayburn what she had been accused of doing and added: "It is not true—I swear to you it is not true. Please help me . . . please. . . .

She signed her name, put the letter in an envelope, and gave it to the Butler.

"Send somebody in a hackney carriage with this to the House of Commons immediately," she ordered. "It is very important!"

"Very good, Miss."

When she had gone back to the Study, Viola picked up her hat trimmed with wistaria, her bag, and her white gloves.

Now she was ready to accompany the Policemen.

Outside the house a Black Maria was waiting, drawn by two horses.

The Policemen helped Viola into it and one of them sat beside her on the hard seat while the other climbed up in front beside the driver.

The horses started off and Viola sat thinking of

what had happened and knowing that this was Lady
Davenport's revenge.

She was well aware that the publicity would not
only react on her but would have a very damaging
effect on Rayburn.

It was quite obvious what construction the newspapers would put on the fact that the fire had been
started by his fiancée in the house of a beautiful woman with whom his name had been associated in the
past.

Viola shut her eyes.

She could see the headlines in the more sensation-
al papers; she could almost hear the sniggering and
the laughter that would be directed not against her
but against Rayburn.

"How could she do this to him ... how could she?"
she asked herself, and knew that she had been right in
comparing Lady Davenport with a snake.

She had planned it all out. She had been determined to strike at the man who had abandoned her
and to hurt him where he was most vulnerable—in his
career.

Nothing could be more disastrous at this time
when everybody in the Government was against
Women's Suffrage than for Rayburn to be involved in
it politically.

And from the personal point of view the drama
would make him the laughing-stock of the social world.

'He will have to resign,' Viola thought despairingly, and she wished she could have died as she had
wanted to when she planted the bomb in his house.

At the Police Station she was charged with arson,
and although she made a statement saying that the
charge against her was untrue she was well aware that
the Police Officer did not believe her.

"You'll go before the Magistrate tomorrow morning," he said gruffly.

His manner showed all too clearly that he had
no sympathy for women who made fools of themselves.

"C-could I have ... bail?" Viola asked.

"If anyone will put up the money on your behalf," the Officer answered. "But in your case, Miss, it'll be high: thirty pounds!"

"I think . . . perhaps . . . someone might do that," Viola answered.

She was taken to the cells without any more discussion on the matter.

To her relief, as it was comparatively early, the drunks and prostitutes who were generally brought in later in the evening had not yet arrived, and so she was alone.

The smell at Bow Street was even worse than it had been at Westminster.

Although she could not help thinking more about Rayburn than herself, Viola knew also how incongruous she looked in her elegant white gown with a large picture hat in a place that smelt of the dregs of humanity, despite the fact that a certain amount of disinfectant had been brushed over the floor.

There was only a hard bench to sit on and a blank wall to stare at, and Viola was haunted by Lady Davenport's face and the tumbling pillar of what had been Rayburn's successful career.

He had worked so hard to achieve his present position and she had learnt from what she had heard other people say that he had done it through sheer ability.

"Your young man will go far," an elderly Statesman had said to her at luncheon.

It seemed now as if it were a century ago.

"I hope so," Viola had answered.

"You mark my words, you will be living at Number 10 Downing Street one of these days," the Statesman had gone on jovially. "But before that I shall look forward to attending some very important Receptions at the Foreign Office."

Perhaps he was being overoptimistic, Viola thought now, but there had been a note of sincerity in his voice that was unmistakable.

When she looked at Rayburn sitting at the head of his own dining-table she had thought there was nothing he could not achieve if he really wanted to.

He was clever and he had too a charm of manner and the aura of leadership which would make people follow him and, where politics were concerned, vote for him.

"How could this have happened? How could Eloise Davenport do this?" Viola asked herself hopelessly, and felt that the whole thing must be a terrible nightmare.

Why had she not realised when the note came from Lady Davenport that it was the poisoned bait of a trap?

Why had not some instinct within her because she loved Rayburn warned her that the woman was dangerous?

"How could I have been so stupid . . . so foolish?" Viola asked accusingly, and knew despairingly that Rayburn could never forgive her.

Now she could see all too clearly that it was an unprecedented action on Lady Davenport's part, considering what she had been in Rayburn's life, to invite his future wife alone to tea with her.

They might have met at a party or with other people, in which case they could both have behaved in a civilised manner, but deliberately to agree to an intimate meeting was to court disaster—and disaster had followed!

It must be growing late, Viola thought after a long while, because there seemed to be no light in the cell and she felt chilled to the bone.

It would have been sensible, she thought, to have brought a coat or a shawl with her, but she had been too bemused when the Policemen fetched her from home to do anything but pick up the hat she had worn to go to Lady Davenport's or to consider how long she might be in the Police Station.

Then a horrifying thought shook her.

Supposing Rayburn decided to leave her there? Supposing he did not wish to be involved further and on receiving her note took no action?

Now Viola began to worry in case she should not have written to him but to her father's Solicitor.

She knew the old man well because she had seen quite a lot of him after her father's death.

He could have come to the Magistrate's Court to bail her out and perhaps that would have been better than involving Rayburn!

But he *was* involved, hopelessly and irretrievably involved!

'Everything I do seems to be wrong,' Viola thought miserably, but at that moment there were lights, the sound of voices, and the rattle of keys.

* * *

A quarter of an hour later, driving away from the Police Station with Rayburn beside her, Viola turned her face to look at him with frightened eyes.

"What happened?" he asked as the brougham started off.

"It is not . . . true! I swear to . . . you it is not . . . true!" Viola cried.

"Why did you go to Lady Davenport's house?"

"She wrote me a letter inviting me to tea with her and I thought it . . . it would be . . . rude to refuse."

Rayburn's lips tightened. He had another opinion on this but he said quietly:

"Tell me exactly what happened."

Viola explained how she had been driven to Belgrave Square.

She remembered most of the conversation she had had with Lady Davenport and how she had said good-bye and been driven home.

"That was all," she finished. "I promise you that nothing else . . . happened. Please . . . please believe me."

"I do believe you," Rayburn said quietly.

Viola felt her heart give a little jerk at the words, then she remembered that while he might believe her, no-one else would.

"What can I do . . . what can I say?" she asked. "Because I live with my Stepmother they will never credit that I am not a Suffragette; that I do not care about the vote."

"It will certainly be hard to prove," Rayburn agreed.

"Then . . . what can we . . . do?" Viola asked in a whisper.

She did not dare to speak of his career, the publicity, all the things which had passed through her mind while she sat in the cell.

He did not answer and at last, as if she could bear the tension no longer, Viola said in a very low voice:

"If I . . . kill myself now . . . as I wanted to do when you . . . found me in your . . . house . . . there could be no . . . trial . . . and perhaps . . . people would just think that I was . . . mad."

Rayburn turned towards her and put his hand over hers.

"You are not to say such things!" he said sharply. "You are never to say or think such things!"

"But . . . I cannot . . . h-hurt you."

"Are you thinking of me?"

"Of course . . . I am . . . thinking of you," she answered, "for I know how this will . . . damage you. That is what she . . . meant to do . . . was it not?"

They both knew to whom she was referring.

"I am afraid it is," Rayburn agreed.

"Then how can we . . . prevent it? How *can* we prevent it?"

His fingers tightened on hers.

"I have an idea," he said, "and because I think you have been through enough this evening I want you to go home and talk about this to no-one."

"I should not tell . . . my Stepmother?"

"No!"

"The servants will have . . . told her that I have been to the . . . Police Station."

"Say it was a mistake. Say they had you muddled with someone else."

Viola looked at him with puzzled eyes.

"You must trust me," he said with a faint smile,

the first he had given her since he had come to the Police Station.

"I would do ... anything if I can help to save you," Viola said. "I am so ... ashamed ... so utterly humiliated and ashamed that I should have brought all this ... trouble upon you."

"I think, if the truth be told, I have brought it upon myself!" Rayburn answered. "Just do as I ask you, Viola."

"Will I have to ... go back in the morning?"

"I hope not," he said gravely, "and because I know you will not sleep until you know what will happen, I will come back to see you before I go to bed."

He saw the uncertainty in her eyes and he said:

"If your household has retired I will just rattle the letter-box, then if you are waiting you can let me in and I will tell you what has occurred."

"I will ... be waiting," Viola said in a very small voice.

She felt the warmth of his fingers, which still held hers, and she said:

"I will be praying ... praying every moment ... all the time ... that you can do ... something ... that you can save yourself from the terrible publicity and all the horrible things that will be ... said. ... I will pray as I have never prayed before!"

"Do that," Rayburn answered, and as he spoke the brougham came to a stop outside the house.

"Try not to worry," he added quietly as the door was opened.

He made no effort to follow Viola onto the pavement and she had the feeling, although he had not said so, that he was in a hurry.

She watched him drive away, then forlornly she went up the steps to the front door.

"Please, God ... please ..." she began, and knew it was a prayer that came from the very depths of her being.

* * *

Rayburn directed his chauffeur to drive to Queen Anne's Gate and to wait.

He was inside the house for less than ten minutes and when he came out they drove to Belgrave Square.

"Her Ladyship has gone up to dress for dinner, Sir," the Butler informed him.

"Then ask her to come down immediately, Hughes."

There was a note in Rayburn's voice which made the Butler look at him in some surprise.

The servants at Belgrave Square knew him well and had always found him courteous and very pleasant to serve.

Rayburn walked up the stairs into the Drawing-Room.

He did not notice, as Viola had done, the fragrance of incense or the overpowering perfume of the lilies with which Eloise Davenport invariably surrounded herself. He was too used to it.

He was standing looking out the window at the far end of the room when she came in wearing one of the long, flowing, transparent negligees in which she had so often received him in her *Boudoir*.

He turned at her entrance and stood looking at her.

The lights had been turned on and although they were discreetly low they turned her red hair into fire, and picked up the glitter in her green eyes.

"Rayburn, this is a surprise!" she exclaimed.

"It is nothing of the sort, as you well know," he replied, and walked across the room to meet her.

They stood looking at each other. Then he said, his voice as hard as the expression in his eyes:

"How could you do anything do damnable?"

"You deserved it!"

"Perhaps," he conceded, "but this does not only concern me."

"You do not suppose I am interested in that milk-faced child to whom you are pretending to be engaged?" Eloise Davenport asked violently.

"To whom I *am* engaged," Rayburn corrected.

"We can of course enjoy ourselves while she is in prison," Lady Davenport said, "and as doubtless it will be for quite some months, you will be lonely without me to keep you company."

"You always told me that you were a vindictive woman," Rayburn Lyle said slowly, "but I did not believe you."

"You will believe me now," Eloise Davenport retorted. "The newspapers are not particularly entranced with your Foreign Policy and they will make the very most of this. I should imagine you will have to resign."

"Undoubtedly, which I am quite prepared to do, if the case ever comes to Court."

"I am ready to give evidence tomorrow," Lady Davenport said sweetly. "I have told the Police so and I have made a statement as to exactly what happened."

She smiled triumphantly.

"You really must have a look at the state of the Morning-Room before you leave. It has completely ruined the carpet. I shall have to buy a new one, and of course the posters with which the room is littered are most convincing."

"I will take your word for it," Rayburn said. "So you intend to go into Court tomorrow morning and perjure yourself on oath?"

"As you perjured yourself a thousand times when you led me to believe that you loved me."

"I never said so in so many words," Rayburn answered, "but I do not intend to discuss what has happened in the past, except in one instance."

"And what is that?" Lady Davenport enquired.

She was supremely confident and sure of herself and Rayburn knew too that standing near to him while they sparred she believed that the fire that had existed between them was not yet finally quenched.

She could not credit that he would fail to be aroused, as he had been aroused a hundred times before, by the seduction of her body and by the provocation of her lips and eyes.

Eloise Davenport was a very conceited woman and she had not the slightest idea that at that mo-

ment Rayburn was hating her as he had never hated
a woman before in his life.

He drew a piece of paper from the inside pocket
of his coat.

"I think I ought to make it quite clear, Eloise," he
said, "that if you denounce Viola in the Police Court
tomorrow morning and she denies your allegations,
which she will do quite truthfully, I shall substantiate
her assertion with this."

"What is that?"

He held the paper out to her.

"It is a copy of a letter you wrote to me about
three months ago after a regrettable little episode re-
garding the Princess Pavavenski when we were staying at Blenheim Palace. I suggest you read it."

For a moment Lady Davenport hesitated, then
she took the paper from him.

It was an extract which she recognised immediately from a letter she had written to Rayburn on
the Palace writing-paper one night after she had accused him of flirting with a very attractive Polish
Princess who was staying there.

> I will kill that woman—murder her or scratch her eyes out
> if you speak to her again. You are mine, and I will not
> share you with anyone. As I lay in your arms last night I
> thought I had never been so happy, but today I have gone
> down into hell and I have come back with the devil's
> poison beneath my finger-nails.
>
> I love you, and I will fight for you with the last
> breath I draw, and if you ever leave me for the Princess
> or any other woman I will make her rue the day, so that
> she will suffer in agony and wish to God she had never
> met you!

Eloise Davenport slowly read the words which
she had written, then she read them again.

"Perhaps the Duke and Duchess of Marlborough
might not be too pleased at being mentioned in such
an unsavoury situation," Rayburn said. "They might
even have to be subpoenaed to prove that we were

their guests, but of course revenge is something in which you specialise, and you must have thought out the consequences."

He spoke very quietly but Eloise Davenport felt as if every word was a blow which demolished her defences and left her vulnerable.

She was well aware that if her letter was read out in Court or published in the newspapers she would be ostracised for the rest of her life.

The Social Code was very clear: "Thou shalt not be found out!" and for the wife of a nobleman to acknowledge that she was committing adultery would be unforgivable.

She stood staring at the piece of paper until she said with a voice that shook:

"You would not dare to produce this!"

"You know very well that I will not hesitate to do so!"

She looked at him wildly and for a moment he thought she was going to defy him. Then she said sullenly:

"Very well, what do you want me to do?"

"You will come with me to the Police Station, retract the statement you made about Viola, and inform them that it was all a mistake. You had better be convincing or they will not accept your explanation."

"And you will get off scot-free."

"So will you."

She looked at him.

Then there was a pause and she looked down again at the piece of paper she held in her hand.

Rayburn waited.

Eloise Davenport raised her eyes.

"Let us tear this up and forget what I have done," she suggested. "Come back to me, Rayburn. I find it impossible to be without you."

The change in her voice and expression was so unexpected that he stared at her with surprise.

"You can get out of this stupid engagement," she went on. "We can be together secretly now, but later . . ."

There was no mistaking the intonation in her voice, but Rayburn had stiffened into a rigidity that seemed to make him taller than he had been before.

"I might have forgiven you for what you tried to do to me," he said slowly, "which was perhaps understandable. But I could never forgive you, Eloise, for trying to harm a young and defenceless girl who is unable to take care of herself."

Lady Davenport uttered a sound that was half frustration and half irritation.

"What can this girl possibly mean to you?" she asked. "She cannot give you the pleasure that we have known together, the excitement, the fire which has consumed us both. Forget her, and let us be happy as we have been before."

"Both your suggestions are impossible," Rayburn replied. "I am sorry, Eloise, if you have been hurt by what was meant to be only a delightful interlude in the lives of both of us. That is all it was, and now it is over."

There was something very final about the way he spoke, but still Eloise Davenport could not believe it.

"Kiss me—touch me," she pleaded, holding out her arms. "You will find that the magic is still there."

Rayburn turned away to walk to the mantelpiece.

"It is too late, Eloise. What has been said and done cannot be undone. Please change your clothes and come with me to the Police Station."

She stood for a moment irresolute, looking at his turned back. Then in a voice that seemed almost strangled with emotion she said bitterly:

"I—hate you! I hate you, Rayburn!"

He did not reply and after a moment she went from the room, leaving him alone.

CHAPTER SEVEN

Viola waited in her bed-room with the door ajar until she heard the Butler turning out the lights in the Hall and then moving with heavy footsteps towards the baize door which led into the servants' quarters.

Now she knew it would be safe for her to go downstairs and wait for Rayburn.

She had felt that the evening would never pass and every hour had seemed drawn out like a century of time.

She had not been forced to make any explanation to her Stepmother, because after Rayburn had left her she remembered that the only person who knew that the Police had called at the house was the old Butler who had been with her father.

She fancied, although she was not sure, that he was fond of her and rather resented her Stepmother's imperious demands and the lack of consideration she showed to the whole household.

Accordingly, when she entered the house Viola said to the old man:

"It was a case of mistaken identity, Bates."

"I thought it must be something like that, Miss Viola," he answered. "You've not been doing anything with those women since you became engaged to Mr. Lyle."

"No, I have tried to keep away from trouble," Viola answered, "so please do not say anything to Her Ladyship when she returns."

If Viola was quiet and had little to say at dinner, Lady Brandon did not notice it.

She was full of the success of the meeting at Wimbledon, and confident that the rally in Oxford the next day would exceed all their hopes for it.

"Why do you not come with me, Viola?" she asked after she had talked for about ten minutes on the subject.

Viola looked surprised.

It was the first time since their return from Croxdale Park that her Stepmother had suggested that she should take part in any Suffragette activity.

"You have not heard Mrs. Pankhurst speak for some time," Lady Brandon went on, "and if you study her methods of holding an audience you will find it useful, I know, in the future."

"*I* shall?" Viola questioned.

Lady Brandon smiled.

"As Rayburn's wife you will be obliged to open innumerable Flower Shows and Bazaars in his constituency, as well as being expected to make speeches when he is not present."

She paused before she went on:

"Besides, I am hoping that when you are married and in a responsible position you will continue to help me. We shall want you on our platforms, Viola."

Viola looked down at her plate.

She had only played with her food and had managed to eat practically nothing. Fortunately her Stepmother did not notice. After a moment she said:

"I am sure . . . that once we are . . . married . . . Rayburn will not wish me to . . . take any part in the . . . Movement."

"Then you will have to persuade him otherwise," Lady Brandon answered briskly. "A clever woman can do anything with the man who is in love with her."

She gave a sharp laugh.

"Not that you are clever, Viola. You never have been. But presumably Rayburn Lyle is in love with you, otherwise there is no possible reason for his wishing to marry you."

There was nothing Viola could say to this and

she was only thankful when her Stepmother changed
the subject and, having put the things ready that she
wished to take with her the following morning, retired to bed.

When the maid helped Viola to undress she
found herself remembering her Stepmother's words.

Of course there was no reason why Rayburn
should want to marry her. She knew that and accepted
it.

At the same time, it still hurt that she had nothing to offer him, and what was more she was a serious
liability.

If by some miracle he did extricate them both
from the trap that Lady Davenport had set, that was
not to say that there would not be other equally
damaging situations waiting for him in the future.

'There is only one thing I can do,' Viola thought
despairingly, and she knew that whatever the cost to
herself she had to set Rayburn free.

The house was now quiet and she went downstairs in her soft slippers without making a sound on
the thick carpet.

She went into her father's Study, turned on two of
the lights, and because the night seemed chill decided
to light the fire.

She was shivering not only because she was wearing nothing but a dressing-gown over her thin night-
gown, but also because she was frightened with a
fear which grew more insistent every moment in case
Rayburn should fail.

He had told her to trust him, but even while she
did so it might prove impossible for him to prevent the
case from going to Court tomorrow morning.

Viola could visualise all too clearly the eager, in-
quisitive faces of the Press as they scribbled down
what was said, and she knew that however much
Rayburn might support her, no-one would believe she
had not lit the fire in Lady Davenport's house out of
jealousy.

It would be said that she had also made it an occasion to proclaim her faith in the Suffragette Movement.

It had been a clever plot, there was no denying that, and she imagined her sentence would be at least two months because she had damaged private property and the Police took a very serious view of those who committed arson.

"Two months! Two months!"

The words seemed to echo round the small Study and Viola found herself praying fervently, as she had been praying all the evening, that Rayburn would find a way of escape.

"Not that I matter," she told herself hastily. "It is he who is important; he who must not be forced to resign because of this wicked, cruel lie."

She glanced at the clock and thought it must have stopped because it seemed to be moving so slowly.

Then she went from the warmth of the Sitting-Room where the fire was flickering over the dry logs and into the Hall.

There was a certain amount of light which came through the windows on each side of the front door from a street-lamp that was just to the left of the steps.

It made the shadows seem very dark, and yet the gas-light had a golden glow about it that was somehow comforting.

Now there was the ticking of the grandfather clock to denote the passing of the minutes.

Viola thought her heart beat in time with it.

At last, when she was beginning to think despairingly that Rayburn must have changed his mind about coming to bring her news, she heard his footsteps outside. He had been wise enough not to stop his brougham directly outside the house.

There was no need for him to rattle the letter-box. Viola opened the door as he came up the steps and as he entered the Hall she put her finger to her lips.

Her Stepmother slept in the front and always alleged that she was a light sleeper.

"It is not so much the traffic which wakes me," she had said a dozen times, "but the sound of voices. How I dislike the cry of the milk-man and those tiresome crossing-sweepers who chatter to each other as soon as it is light."

Viola shut the door behind Rayburn and he set his hat down on a chair and followed her into the Study, which was at the back of the house, where she knew they would not be overheard.

She opened the door and as she entered the room behind him she stood, unable to move any further, her eyes dark and purple, fixed on his.

He looked at her for the first time since his arrival and thought she looked more like a violet than ever.

Her dressing-gown was of white silk trimmed with lace and buttoned down the front from her neck to her toes. Her fair hair fell on either side of her small face and was much longer than he had imagined it would be.

She looked very young, very sensitive, and very vulnerable.

Then he smiled and it seemed to Viola as if the whole room became flooded with light.

"What has . . . happened?" she whispered.

He could hardly hear the question, and he saw that her lips were trembling.

"It is all right," he said softly. "It is quite all right."

She put her hands up to her face as if something had cracked inside her and the tears came pouring down her cheeks.

He crossed the room to put his arms round her and hold her very close against him.

"It is all right," he said again. "I know the waiting must have been intolerable, but I could not get here any sooner."

She was crying against his shoulder, but he knew that she was listening.

"Lady Davenport has withdrawn all the charges against you. The Police have accepted that it was a

misunderstanding and nothing more will be heard
about the whole episode."

He felt her body tremble in his arms and he said
gently:

"There will be no publicity, no-one except you
and me will ever know what happened, and we must
try to forget it."

"No . . . one will . . . know?"

"No-one."

"But . . . how . . . ?"

"Does it matter?" he asked. "You are free, there
will be no scandal, no gossip—all you have to do is to
forget you ever met Lady Davenport."

For the moment his voice sharpened.

He did not realise what a superhuman effort it
was for Viola to withdraw herself from his arms.

Her cheeks were wet with tears and for the moment she made no effort to wipe them away.

"There is . . . something I have to . . . say to . . .
you."

"And I have a lot to say to you," Rayburn answered. "But you shall speak first."

"You-you have been very . . . kind," Viola said,
"and I know that you . . . saved me from a terrifying
situation by announcing our engagement. But it may
. . . damage you and . . . end your career in politics."

Rayburn's eyes were on her face, but he did not
speak.

"This time you have been able to prevent . . . L-
Lady Davenport from making trouble for us," Viola
went on, "but there is still my Stepmother . . . who will
try to involve me in the Movement . . . whatever I say
or do."

"What are you suggesting?" Rayburn asked.

"That we should . . . end our . . . pretended engagement and that you should be . . . free of me."

As she spoke, she felt as if she were cutting off
an arm or a leg or—worse—removing her heart from
her body.

There would be nothing left for her to live for, she
thought, nothing to look forward to or care about once

he had gone, but whatever the cost to herself she must save him.

"You are thinking of me?" Rayburn asked.

"Of course I am thinking of you," Viola answered. "You are so clever, and you have so much to give to the world. You are needed by the whole country. How can I let you . . . risk all that just to help me avoid . . . Lord Croxdale?"

"And supposing he continues to pursue you?" Rayburn asked.

He did not miss the little tremor that went through Viola or the fact that her fingers trembled and she twisted them together.

"I . . . I will manage . . . somehow," she said bravely. "Perhaps I can go away to . . . Scotland, or somewhere where he will not find me."

"Do you think that would make you happy?"

For a moment she was tempted to tell him the truth, that she would never be happy without him, that the whole world would be dark, empty, and frightening without him beside her.

Then she lifted her small chin and said:

"You must no longer . . . concern yourself with . . . me . . . but think about . . . yourself."

"That is exactly what I intend to do, Viola," Rayburn said. "But now I want to tell you what I discovered when I left you this evening to try to save us both from the very uncomfortable predicament in which we found ourselves."

Viola gave him a fleeting glance from under her wet eye-lashes. He was looking at her and she suddenly became conscious of her tear-drenched cheeks.

She tried to wipe them away with the back of her hand but as she did so Rayburn smiled and offered her his handkerchief. It was of very soft linen and smelt of lavender.

Because it was his, and because of his consideration for her, she felt her love welling up inside her like a warm wave which made her want to cry again.

She wiped her eyes fiercely, then crushing the handkerchief in her hands she looked at him again and hoped that he would not think her more tiresome than usual because she had cried against him.

"Now you look exactly like a violet after a shower of rain," he said.

As if his words made her conscious of her appearance, Viola touched her dressing-gown nervously.

"I . . . I am sorry you should . . . see me like . . . this," she said, "but the maid who helped me . . . undress would have thought it . . . strange if I had tried to . . . remain in my . . . evening-gown."

"I am not complaining," Rayburn answered. "If you want the truth, you look very lovely—far more lovely than I have ever seen you look before."

His words brought a touch of colour to Viola's cheeks. Then he said:

"As I have a lot to say to you, shall we say it in a more comfortable fashion?"

Because he expected it of her, Viola sat down on the sofa.

He sat beside her, nearer than she had expected, and she felt a little thrill go through her because their shoulders were touching. Then she told herself that he was going to accept her suggestion and after tonight they would never meet again.

It was an indescribable agony to wait for him to confirm in words what she expected he would say.

"I told you that I discovered something about myself when I left you this evening," Rayburn began. "It was in fact something I have known for a long time, but had not actually put into words."

Since he seemed to be waiting for her to speak, Viola asked:

"What . . . did you discover?"

"I discovered that I love you!"

He felt Viola stiffen for a moment. Then she turned her head to look at him as if she could not have heard him aright.

"It is true," he said gently. "I love you, my darling, but I did not really know until tonight, when I had to rescue you for the third time, how much you mean to me and that it would be impossible for me to go on living without you."

He saw her eyes widen and a light that seemed to transform her whole face shone from them dazzlingly.

He put his arms round her and drew her close against him.

"It . . . cannot be . . . true!" Viola murmured.

"It is true!" he insisted, and his lips found hers.

He had never known that anything could be so soft, so sweet, so innocent. Then as he felt a quiver of excitement go through her and her whole body seemed to move closer to him his mouth became more demanding, more insistent.

For Viola it was a moment of surprise which made her incapable of thought, until as Rayburn's lips took possession of hers she felt as if the whole world vanished and there was nothing but the wonder of his arms and him.

As the pressure on her lips increased, she felt that all her past fears had vanished and all that she had ever longed for but had seemed out of reach became part of the rapture of his kiss.

There was something spiritual and holy about it, as if it was part of her prayers, and yet at the same time it was an excitement which ran through her body, making her feel that she had come alive and was part of life itself.

Time stood still and there was only an eternity of being one with each other before Rayburn raised his head.

"I love you, my precious little violet," he said. "Now—tell me that you love me too."

"I do love you!" Viola replied. "I love you with . . . all my heart and soul, but because I love you so . . . desperately I cannot . . . I must not . . . hurt you."

"It would hurt me only if you should leave me and refuse to marry me," Rayburn said, "and that, my darling, is the true solution to the problem."

"But your career . . . there must be no . . . publicity that would . . . damage you."

"Once you are my wife I doubt if anybody would do anything to try to harm us," Rayburn said.

Then he added with laughter in his voice:

"And I promise you I will not allow you to vote for anything except love!"

"Do you think I would want to do . . . anything else?" Viola asked. "But are you sure . . . quite sure?"

"I am quite sure!" Rayburn said firmly. "And the only way that you can make me feel happy and secure from the 'barbs and arrows' of our enemies is by becoming my wife."

"I want that above all things," Viola said, "but I never thought that you could ever . . . love me. I have nothing to . . . offer you."

Rayburn smiled and his arms tightened about her.

"You will be giving me everything I want in my wife," he answered. "I thought at first that I felt sorry for you and must protect you because you were pathetic and child-like. But then I knew that I did not only want to protect you, but to possess you—to make sure you were mine—always and forever!"

Viola drew in a deep breath and he thought as she looked up him that he had never seen a woman look so radiant.

"I am very stupid in some ways," she said humbly, "and I am not glamorous or sophisticated like your other . . . friends."

"Those are not the things I want in my wife," Rayburn said. "That was what I found in the women who entertained me and amused me for a short while."

He kissed her forehead.

"But I do not think you, my darling, can do without me, and I know I cannot do without you."

"I want to help you . . . I want to look after you . . . and I want to . . . love you," Viola said.

There was a passionate note in her voice which made Rayburn seek her lips and once again she could think of nothing but him.

He kissed her until the breath came quickly, then

he kissed her eyes, still wet from her tears, her cheeks, and the softness of her neck.

He had never thought anything could be so entrancingly different, in a way he could not explain, from anything he had ever done before.

It was in fact as if he touched a flower and drew from it not the flaming passion he had always aroused in women before, but a spiritual substance which unexpectedly he found in himself.

It was as if Viola revived the ideals and the aspirations which had been his when he was very young and which had been forgotten in his determination to achieve political success.

Now he knew that because she was pure and good in the real meaning of the word, he too would find again the chivalry, the nobility, and the vision which had once been a very vital part of his character.

"I love ... you ... I love you ..." Viola whispered.

She did not understand the rapture he evoked in her. She only knew it was what she had dreamt love would be, only more wonderful, more perfect.

"I have so much to say to you, so much to teach you, my precious," he said a little unsteadily as he looked down into her adoring eyes, "and I am determined that you shall no longer be subjected to the dangers of this house or of the world outside. How soon will you marry me?"

"Can it be really ... soon?" Viola asked.

"As soon as you are ready."

"I can be ready now ... or tomorrow!"

Rayburn laughed and pulled her close.

"That, my sweet little love, is exactly the right answer, but I think we will have to make it the day after. I shall have to get a Special Licence and we can be married in the crypt of the House of Commons so that there will be no publicity, and I suggest we tell no-one, not even your Stepmother, until it is over."

"Could we really do that?" Viola asked. "It would be wonderful ... the most wonderful way to be married ... if I could be alone with you and ... God. ..."

She said the last word a little shyly, for she was afraid that Rayburn might think she was being over-emotional.

He put his fingers under her chin and turned her face up to his.

"Were you praying, as you said you would, when I left this evening?"

"I prayed all the time."

"I felt your prayers were with me," he said quietly. "In fact I was sure you were helping me, telling me the right things to say and do."

He drew in a deep breath and went on:

"There is something about you, my precious little one, which makes me feel as if I carry you in my heart like a talisman. You will always be there, guiding me, helping me towards everything that is fine and good for the rest of our lives."

Viola gave a little cry of sheer joy.

"It is what I wish to do," she said. "But you are so . . . magnificent, so . . . wonderful, that I thought I was too . . . insignificant to be of any consequence in your life."

"You are everything that matters," Rayburn said. "Everything that a man wants in his home and in his personal world, which should always be private and apart from his public one."

His arms tightened and he said:

"The inspiration you give me, the love I see in your eyes, and the prayer on your lips is feminine and very wonderful."

His voice deepened as he went on:

"No vote, no Act of Parliament, no alteration of a woman's status could make you more important to me than you are already just by being a woman."

"I want to be . . . your woman," Viola whispered.

Then because she was shy she hid her face against his neck.

"You will be my woman and my wife," Rayburn replied, "and I will love you, adore you, and worship you for the rest of our lives!"

He felt Viola give a deep sigh of happiness, before he continued:

"You are mine, Viola, my very own special, secret little white violet, needing shelter from the harshness and cruelty of storms, but exquisite, fragrant, and perfect to the person who is privileged to find you."

"As you . . . found me," Viola whispered.

"And having found you I will never let you go, my darling. You need never be afraid again."

"I will never be afraid when I am close to you," Viola said. "I love you! Oh, Rayburn, I love you with my whole being! I cannot tell you in words how great my love is, but I know that it touches Heaven itself!"

"I believe that, too," Rayburn replied, "and we must never, my precious, lose our belief in our love or our belief in ourselves!"

"I believe in . . . you," Viola whispered.

"And I believe I will make you happy," he answered.

He sought her lips, and as his mouth, passionate, demanding, and insistent, held her captive she knew that he carried her into a special Heaven of their own where there was no fear, no anxiety, but only a love which was a part of God.

ABOUT THE AUTHOR

BARBARA CARTLAND, the celebrated romantic author, historian, playwright, lecturer, political speaker and television personality, has now written over 150 books. Miss Cartland has had a number of historical books published and several biographical ones, including that of her brother, Major Ronald Cartland, who was the first Member of Parliament to be killed in the War. This book had a Foreword by Sir Winston Churchill.

In private life, Barbara Cartland, who is a Dame of the Order of St. John of Jerusalem, has fought for better conditions and salaries for Midwives and Nurses. As President of the Royal College of Midwives (Hertfordshire Branch), she has been invested with the first Badge of Office ever given in Great Britain, which was subscribed to by the Midwives themselves. She has also championed the cause for old people and founded the first Romany Gypsy Camp in the world.

Barbara Cartland is deeply interested in Vitamin Therapy and is President of the British National Association for Health.

Barbara Cartland

The world's bestselling author of romantic fiction. Her stories are always captivating tales of intrigue, adventure and love.

☐	THE TEARS OF LOVE	2148	$1.25
☐	THE DEVIL IN LOVE	2149	$1.25
☐	THE ELUSIVE EARL	2436	$1.25
☐	THE BORED BRIDEGROOM	6381	$1.25
☐	JOURNEY TO PARADISE	6383	$1.25
☐	THE PENNILESS PEER	6387	$1.25
☐	NO DARKNESS FOR LOVE	6427	$1.25
☐	THE LITTLE ADVENTURE	6428	$1.25
☐	LESSONS IN LOVE	6431	$1.25
☐	THE DARING DECEPTION	6435	$1.25
☐	CASTLE OF FEAR	8103	$1.25
☐	THE GLITTERING LIGHTS	8104	$1.25
☐	A SWORD TO THE HEART	8105	$1.25
☐	THE MAGNIFICENT MARRIAGE	8166	$1.25
☐	THE RUTHLESS RAKE	8240	$1.25
☐	THE DANGEROUS DANDY	8280	$1.25
☐	THE WICKED MARQUIS	8467	$1.25
☐	LOVE IS INNOCENT	8505	$1.25
☐	THE FRIGHTENED BRIDE	8780	$1.25
☐	THE FLAME IS LOVE	8887	$1.25

Buy them at your local bookseller or use this handy coupon:

Barbara Cartland

The world's bestselling author of romantic fiction. Her stories are always captivating tales of intrigue, adventure and love.

☐	THE CRUEL COUNT	2128	$1.25
☐	CALL OF THE HEART	2140	$1.25
☐	AS EAGLES FLY	2147	$1.25
☐	THE MASK OF LOVE	2366	$1.25
☐	AN ARROW OF LOVE	2426	$1.25
☐	A GAMBLE WITH HEARTS	2430	$1.25
☐	A KISS FOR THE KING	2433	$1.25
☐	A FRAME OF DREAMS	2434	$1.25
☐	THE FRAGRANT FLOWER	2435	$1.25
☐	MOON OVER EDEN	2437	$1.25
☐	THE GOLDEN ILLUSION	2449	$1.25
☐	FIRE ON THE SNOW	2450	$1.25
☐	THE HUSBAND HUNTERS	2461	$1.25
☐	THE SHADOW OF SIN	6430	$1.25
☐	SAY YES, SAMANTHA	7834	$1.25
☐	THE KARMA OF LOVE	8106	$1.25
☐	BEWITCHED	8630	$1.25
☐	THE IMPETUOUS DUCHESS	8705	$1.25

Buy them at your local bookseller or use this handy coupon: